ACKNOWLEDGEMENT

A special thank you goes out to Joseph Wambaugh, the King of the police novel, who is able to combine a fictional story with real police situations and was the inspiration for this book.

CHAPTER ONE

It was another beautiful Los Angeles morning as Matt walked the campus of UCLA. He marveled at the silence as the students were preparing for their final exams. Matt was saddened to think about the fact that his college life was coming to a close and now he would have to actually go out and face the world.

Born Matthew Wellington Miles, his parents, who had immigrated to the United States from Northern Ireland, committed that they would do whatever it took to assure their son received a college education and they both worked hard at their blue collar jobs to make that happen.

On his high school graduation day his parents told him that he had a choice. He could attend college and they would pay for all his expenses or he could move out of the house and begin his own life. The very next day Matt was in the Admissions Office of UCLA perusing choices of majors to decide which looked like the easiest. Matt decided on Criminal Justice because he was a long time fan of the TV show CSI and he could breeze through with what he had learned from the show.

Matt's idea of studying was being at beach where he could show off his buff six foot frame in a skimpy bathing suit. He reveled on the looks he received from both the males and the females, even though he was not sure how to react to admiration from other males. Matt had the physical appearance of an athlete, but never attempted sports because it would require too much effort and commitment.

Matt had scored one hundred and fifteen on the IQ test, but he never developed the work ethic that his parents needed to pay for his schooling. Now he was going to actually have to get out and find a job and become a real adult which was not a pleasing thought at all. He liked having his dinner cooked for him and not having to do his own laundry. His parents, on the other hand, relished in the thought that they would have their lives back now that they had given him every opportunity to succeed.

Matt had broached the subject of remaining in school to get his Masters Degree and maybe even a Ph.D., but his parents said they could not pay for any more education and that Matt was on his own after graduation.

As Matt turned to enter the examination room he was much less concerned about the Advanced Psychology test he was about to take than he was about how he could use what he learned to convince his parents to continue to support him.

Walking away from the campus for the very last time caused Matt to be morose and depressed. He had reached a point where he would have to develop his own life and would not be able to relax and play as much. He did not even have the energy to drive to the beach to show off to the beach bunnies and beach bums that frequent there.

While driving home he developed a plan that he thought might work. He would begin a nationwide search for police officer vacancies in the hope that his parents would want to keep him close to them and let him get a few more years at home where he could be supported and have the freedom he so desired.

As soon as he arrived home he went to his room and turned on the computer. He did a search of the internet for law enforcement employment opportunities and immediately found that New York City, Atlanta and Cincinnati were hiring. The thought of being a cop in New York where he would be one of thirty-five thousand other cops immediately turned him off. Atlanta was a bit more enticing because of their weather, but that might be something his parents would encourage and he definitely did not want them to like the idea. He clicked on the link to Cincinnati because it was in the Midwest and least likely to have his parents approval.

Cincinnati, like most major cities who are hiring, offered out of state applicants and opportunity to complete the testing process in two consecutive days to save expenses to the applicant. In order for Matt to sell the idea to his parents that he really wanted to go there to work he would have to do some research on what Cincinnati was and is.

Matt found that Cincinnati is an old German city of just over three hundred thousand which sits on the border of Kentucky and Indiana. It is called the Queen City and is famous for its seven hills. When he found that the new Police Chief spent twenty-six years as a cop in LA, he could tell his parents that he was attracted to the department because of that reason. Cincinnati is also the site of the second largest Oktoberfest in the world each fall and has both professional football and baseball franchises. Matt learned in his research that Cincinnati had the first professional fire department in the country and the third professional police department. Cincinnati has just over one thousand sworn police officers.

Using the techniques that he learned in college psychology classes, Matt figured the more it looked like he wanted to apply with Cincinnati, the less likely his parents were to support it. He would present his package to his parents at the dinner table where he believed that they would be the most vulnerable. He was unaware that his parents had been praying for this day to come so that they could live their own lives without him to intrude.

His mother had made his favorite dish of fish and chips to celebrate the completion of his college career and he sat and savored the food as he contemplated the right moment to drop his bombshell on them. They were sipping tea at the end of the meal when he decided to make his pitch to them. He told his parents that after searching the internet for hours to find employment opportunities, he found that the Cincinnati Police were hiring. Of course, since he did not have the funds to pay the costs of the airfare and hotel for two days, he would not be able to actually apply for the position. He told them he was going to start the exhaustive search of local police agencies to gain employment.

Matt almost fell off the dining room chair when his father told him that his parents had set aside money for him to be able to make a job interview in another part of the country and that Cincinnati sounded like a good place to start. Matt went back to his room to complete the application because he was stuck with his decision to try to play his parents.

The application was relatively simple to fill out. His parents told him that as long as he remained in school he would not have to find a job, so he had no employment history. Also, when his parents bought him the Mustang convertible he drives he was told that it would be taken away after the first traffic citation he received. When Matt submitted the application online, he was sent a message that his testing would be scheduled and he would be notified by electronic mail of the dates he needed to be in Cincinnati.

Having no income, other than the allowance that his parents provided left him little money for things other than gasoline for his car and almost no options with respect to dating. He would only be able to date if the girl would pay half the expenses or, even better, pay for the date herself.

Memories of being spoiled by a wealthy, beautiful girl from the hills of LA flooded his mind. What was her name? Well, that escaped him at the moment but not the depth of those loaded pockets or the feel of those voluptuous curves. On several occasions she treated Matt to meals, movies and other outings, but on one spectacularly beautiful summer afternoon she treated him to a whole new world. Innocently enough, he'd accepted an invitation to her house not sure quite what to expect. When he arrived and learned her parents were out of town, his excitement began to build. When her "tour of the house" led straight to the in-ground pool out back, his interest really piqued. And when she stripped naked and told him to follow suit, Matt's nerves jangled like pots on a line being banged by metal spoons.
There was an eight-foot privacy fence surrounding the property and they were above the neighboring homes...but still. Matt was filled

with the anxiety of the unexpected, the thrill of being desired and the rush of taking such a risk.

Seeing his temporary paralysis from all these conflicting emotions, his lovely hostess – Shelby that was her name! – unbuckled his pants, her fingertips slowly gliding along the waistband and gently brushing his skin. The way she moved while performing so ordinary a task, her hands gracefully flowing, her rear end firming as she bent lower, Matt was more and more intoxicated by this goddess focusing all her attention on him. If she could ignite this kind of fire just taking off his clothes, he wasn't sure he could survive what she might do to his body! As she pushed his khakis to the ground, she took extra care to caress his lean thighs and calves. Matt trembled and gasped, only then realizing he'd been holding his breath since the moment she told him to undress.

Once he was completely naked, he hurriedly slid into the comfort and security of the cool water and immediately felt more confident about this set-up he'd stumbled into. Here, his athleticism and love of being in the water gave him a stronger sense of control and eased his embarrassment. Shelby then joined him, and the two actually enjoyed several minutes of splashing around in luxury and seclusion.

"Why don't you hop up on the edge of the pool and let your feet dangle in the water, Matt?"

"Oh, ok," he replied, completely missing the sly, seductive smile Shelby gave him when she asked.

Clueless and curious, he turned and sat facing Shelby. Her radiant smile and sparkling eyes mesmerized him. Then he noticed where her eyes were trained and understood the extra glint that wasn't there before. He had a massive erection from their water foreplay, and it was all Shelby could do not to salivate while she stared. Pushing his shoulders back until he was prone, she took him deeply into her mouth masterfully riding him up and down while pressing her thumb on the underside of his penis. The pressure from the teasing caused him to throb uncontrollably and seemed to make the sun shine brighter, the water get cooler and the handful of her hair he was grasping feel silkier. Finally overcome with passion and anticipation herself, Shelby let go and Matt released like he never imagined he could ever do. His moans and shudders made her smile, a smile imprinted on his brain like the gray matter itself.
That was the last time he ever saw her.

***

Matt had two weeks until his graduation ceremony, so he wanted to spend as much of that at the beach as possible. He was unsure of what the future might hold for him, but he was sure that he would no longer have the time to spend with the bunnies and bums that frequented the beach.

Suddenly, Matthew Wellington Miles life was moving much faster than he anticipated.

CHAPTER TWO

Matt rolled out of the bed after a long night at the beach and immediately turned on his computer. There were four messages in his inbox, one of which was from the Cincinnati Civil Service Commission.

He opened the e-mail and found instructions and found the dates of his testing. His face immediately lit up as it was scheduled for the same day as his graduation. He eagerly printed it out so he could take this to his parents and get out from under the mess he had created. His parents were eating breakfast at the kitchen table and he put on his puppy-dog face to break the bad news to them.

He truly hoped that they would tell him to take his time and look elsewhere when his mother told him to contact the Cincinnati Civil Service Commission at the number on the instructions and they would understand and change the date. Once again Matt's best efforts to employ psychology had failed him. He went back to his room to make the call, hoping that Cincinnati would not change the dates.

The lady at the Civil Service Office told him that they completely understood the importance of his graduation ceremony and would change the date to two days after. Matt begrudgingly walked back downstairs and gave his parents the news. His mother was on the telephone within minutes making the reservation for the flight, hotel and rental car.

Matt saw his graduation as a sad rather than a celebratory event because it would mean the end of his free ride. He sat through the ceremony with a stoic look on his face and almost grudgingly accepted the diploma that was handed to him.

The next day his parents drove him to the airport so he would not have to leave his car there. His mother had carefully packed him a suit for the interview, casual outfit for the written examination, psychological and polygraph tests, and a matched set of workout clothes for the physical agility and run that he would be required to complete. She even packed energy snacks to help him during and after the tests.

Once the plane was airborne Matt opened the folder he had brought which contained the letter from Cincinnati, which said:

Thank you for applying to become a Cincinnati Police officer. Your itinerary is listed below.

Day one
8:00am-10:00am   Written examination
1030am-1130am   Physical examination

1:00 pm-2:00pm   Physical Agility testing

2:30pm –4:00pm Fitness run and tests

Day two

8:00am-9:30am   Polygraph examination

9:30am-12:00pm Psychological Testing

1:00pm-3:00pm   Psychological Interview

3:00pm-4:00pm   Oral Interview

We wish you success in your testing process.

Sincerely,

Cincinnati Civil Service Commission

Matt had no real concern about the written examination, as he had always been a good test-taker. The letter from Cincinnati told him that the physical agility portion would consist of an obstacle course and the pulling of one hundred fifty pounds a measured distance. The run would be one and one half miles and would have to be completed within a specified time. The rest of the fitness testing would consist of pull-ups, sit-ups and push-ups and would occur immediately after the run to measure his cardio stamina. No information was provided as to the contents of the day two itinerary.

Television crime shows carried little content on a polygraph test and Matt was concerned about how that was going to work. His only contact with the Lie Detector was an NCIS episode where the lead character is given a lie detector and gets up and walks out on it. From his college classes Matt felt comfortable about taking the written and oral psychological tests and the Oral Interview should be a cakewalk.

As the plane touched down, Matt was amazed to learn that the Airport was not only not in Cincinnati; it is not even in Ohio. When he approached the terminal he noticed how small the airport is comparative to LAX and went to find the rental car company that his parents had paid for in advance for him. He asked the woman at the counter how to get to the Hyatt Hotel in downtown and was told that it was a fifteen mile drive north on the Interstate.

Matt got into the rental car and followed the signs directing him into Cincinnati. He crossed over a bridge between Ohio and Kentucky and saw the football stadium and the baseball stadium that house the Reds and Bengals.

Matt arrived at the hotel and was amazed by how clean the downtown area of Cincinnati is. He was in a hotel across from the centerpiece of downtown Cincinnati that is called Fountain Square at Fifth and Vine Streets. In the center of the square is a granite fountain and there were people congregated on the walls enjoying their lunch.

Matt's parents had given him two hundred and fifty dollars in cash to cover his meals and other expenses and his room offered a great view of the fountain. He took notice that the cops in Cincinnati wear white shirts and white vinyl hats with royal blue pants with portable radios attached to the upper area of their shirts.

Having not eaten anything since breakfast he walked out of the hotel and found a little hole in the wall called the Orange Bar. They had hot dogs, something called Brats, and something calls Metts. When he asked the clerk what those were, the clerk told him german sausage. He ordered a Brat and chips with an orange drink and walked onto Fountain Square where the sun was beating down on the workers who were relaxing during their lunch breaks. He was very impressed with the fact that people in a downtown environment were so relaxed and unconcerned about being assaulted or robbed, unlike downtown LA. He looked at the high rise buildings that were a combination of old and new like the twin towers of Procter and Gamble and the Fifth-Third Tower building. On the opposite side of Vine there was an old high rise that had the name Carew Tower on its wall.

Matt decided to walk back to the hotel trying to take in everything he could about this city. He saw the white Ford Crown Victorias with blue lettering POLICE down the side and Cincinnati on the rear quarter panel driving up and down and saw a motorcycle with red and blue flashing lights, its rider wearing leather boots and a helmet. He wanted to get a nap and then take in some of the nightlife of this City before beginning the testing tomorrow.

Matt decided instead to go the exercise room to work off the long flight then went back to his room to shower. He returned to the lobby where he asked the bellman where to find a meal that would not be expensive. He told the bellman he had just arrived from Los Angeles and would only be in town for two days. The guy looked at Matt and said that Matt needed to try Cincinnati chili and that there was a place called Skyline Chili less than two blocks from the hotel. Matt walked up the street to Seventh and Vine and found the restaurant that looked like a stainless steel diner to him. He sat down at a table and the waitress, who looked like she was sixteen, asked for his order.

Matt looked at the young girl and told her he was in town for only a couple of days from the west coast and she should tell him what he wanted for dinner. She smiled meekly and said he should order a five way and a cheese coney. Matt asked her what a five way consisted of and she told him chili, spaghetti, cheese, onion and beans. She returned to the table in less than five minutes with the food. Matt looked at the miniature hot dog inside a miniature bun smothered with chili and cheese and a small amount of onion on top. Three bites and it was gone. Next he tasted the five-way which came on an oblong plate, but the waitress would not allow him to eat it without first putting a bib around his neck which had Matt embarrassed until the first spill of the thin liquid that Cincinnati called chili. After he had the first bite, he added some hot sauce from a bottle of RedHot on the table and sipped on his Pepsi to cool his mouth from the burning sensation. He thought to himself, "I could learn to like this!"

Matt slowly walked back toward the hotel taking in all the sights and sounds of downtown Cincinnati as the workers were rushing to go home after another work day. It was a peaceful chaos that he was witnessing and it was actually refreshing and different from the world of the west coast.

When he returned to the hotel he stopped and thanked the bellman for the tip on dinner and pressed a five dollar bill into the bellman's hand. He looked at the young bellman and asked if there was some sight within walking distance because he had an early start to the day tomorrow. The bellman smiled and told him to wait until dark and go down to the river to Cincinnati's newest park. Smale Park that was named for the retired President of Procter and Gamble and featured a waterfall down a rock wall with pastel colors behind the water.

Matt waited until a little after nine o'clock before walking down to the park which was only about ten blocks from the hotel. There were people quietly milling about and he watched the Ohio River as a barge crept along at a snail's pace and the backdrop of the Kentucky skyline. He could see Great American Ballpark and Paul Brown Stadium off in the distance and a facility called US Bank Arena which looked like some kind of indoor center. The weather in Cincinnati had been absolutely perfect for his arrival. He wanted to get a good night's sleep because the next day would be a long one, so he decided it was time to walk back to the hotel.

As Matt was walking up Walnut Street from the river, he heard what sounded like a moan coming from an alleyway off to his right. He looked down the alley just in time to see a man running away from him and saw what looked like a body in the middle of the alley. Matt decided not to enter the alley because he learned from watching CSI not to contaminate a crime scene.

He quickly reached into his pocket and grabbed his cell phone to call 9-1-1. He told the female dispatcher he was in Cincinnati from Los Angeles for the Police Department testing and that he saw a man running away in an alley between fourth and fifth on Walnut. Within seconds after he hung up with the police dispatcher, he heard sirens wailing from all directions. Police cars with lights flashing came the wrong way on the one-way street, screeching to a halt where he was standing. As the first two officers approached him, Matt pointed into the alley where it appeared someone was on the ground. Matt watched as the officers flashlights showed upon a young woman wearing a light colored blouse and a dark colored skirt was lifeless on the ground. From the distance he was away, he could see her long brown hair matted from the blood and blood on her blouse as well. One of the officers came back to him and asked for a description of the man who Matt saw running away. Matt was only able to tell him that the guy was a male, about five feet ten inches, average build, with dark color hair. The suspect was wearing a dark color long sleeve shirt, dark pants and had to be wearing gym shoes. The officer, who had been on the job about three years asked him how he knew that the guy had on gym shoes. Matt told the officer that there was no sound of the shoes hitting the pavement and the smoothness of the run meant that he had to be wearing rubber soled sneakers.

The officer pressed the button on his shoulder microphone and broadcast the description out to all of the officers in the vicinity.

The first two officers had already put up crime scene tape, but Matt was astonished that officers kept arriving and walking up to the body and contaminating the crime scene. Paramedics arrived shortly after and pronounced the woman dead, leaving her lay there until the Coroner's office could be notified to respond.

Because the Homicide Unit of the Cincinnati Police is only four blocks from where the crime occurred, detectives were there within minutes. That included a Lieutenant, two Sergeants, and four detectives. The Crime Scene van was on scene in fifteen minutes. One of the Sergeants approached Matt and asked him to repeat everything he had told dispatch and the first arriving officers.

Matt went through everything he said and saw when the Sergeant asked if he had seen the face or the race of the suspect. Matt wondered why no one else had asked those questions before. Matt explained that the guy was running in the opposite direction when Matt first saw him and there was very little light in the alley.

The Sergeant asked Matt to accompany him to the Criminal Investigation Unit a few blocks away so that they could get a statement from him. It was now just past eleven o'clock and Matt had to be at the testing site prior to eight in the morning. He told the Sergeant about his dilemma since he had to be at the police academy first thing.

The Sergeant, who had more than thirty years on the job, took Matt's name and hotel information and told Matt they would contact him at the police academy or after the testing day to get his statement in writing. The Sergeant then offered Matt a ride back to his hotel which Matt gladly accepted.

Matt went straight to his room and then the moment caught up with him as he began to shake uncontrollably. He had never witnessed a crime of any kind before and he knew he would not be sleeping well tonight.

***

Matt really did not want to answer the room phone when it rang at six fifteen, but he dutifully thanked the desk clerk and got up to take his shower. He put on the casual outfit that his mother had packed specifically for the first sessions of the testing which consisted of a short sleeve pale blue shirt and khaki pants. He chose his running shoes to finish the outfit and put his workout clothes in the gym bag his mother had packed for him.

Matt went down to the coffee shop where he ordered a cheese Danish and a cup of coffee. He wanted to eat light so that he would not be overly sluggish in the test, something that he learned in a college class. He was glad to have found out that the Police Academy facility was only a three mile drive from the hotel at what used to be called Spinney Field which was the training field for the Cincinnati Bengal professional football team.

Matt pulled into the parking lot which only had a few marked police cars in it and several unmarked cars which he assumed were owned by the employees. He walked in the front door and approached the reception desk where a young woman was working on her computer. He waited until she completed whatever it was she was working on and told her he was there for the Police Applicant testing. Without speaking a word the woman got out of her chair and led Matt to an empty classroom and simply pointed toward a desk. Matt walked over to the desk and prepared to sit down when he heard the door close behind him and the receptionist was gone.

Matt sat quietly in the empty room for about ten minutes when a slightly overweight woman who looked to be in her fifties came into the room with an armload of papers. Matt could tell by her body language and facial expression that she was not at all happy being given the task of babysitting another wannabe cop.

The woman quietly set down her papers on the instructor desk and introduced herself to Matt as Mrs. Madelyn Quently of the Cincinnati Civil Service Commission. Her voice was stern and terse as she began giving the instructions about the testing procedure. The testing would consist of two phases. The first phase was a general intelligence test which covered things such as vocabulary, spelling, composition and problem solving. There would be a one hour time limit on this phase. The second phase would test his memory and there would be a thirty minute time limit on this phase.

Matt would not be allowed to have anything on the desk other than what Mrs. Quently placed there. That included two number 2 pencils, the test booklet, an answer sheet, and loose leaf paper. Matt would not be allowed to write anything in or on the test booklet. Mrs. Quently told Matt to take no more than one minute per question, and to skip over any questions he had difficulty with. If, at the end of the test period, there was any time left Matt could return to the unanswered questions and complete them. She also suggested that Matt save a few minutes to review random questions to assure that the answer marked was intended for the question asked.

Mrs. Quently asked if Matt had any questions of her because once the test procedure started she was not allowed to say anything to him. When Matt told her he had no questions, she told him to open the book and that the clock started now.

Matt opened the booklet and perused the first page of questions without picking up the pencil. It became clear that the questions were written at a reading level that a child would be able to read and understand, so this was going to be a breeze for him.

Almost half of the time had expired when there was a knock at the classroom door. Matt could see it was the same receptionist who brought him to the classroom as Mrs. Quently walked to the door. There was whispering between the two and Matt could see some look of disbelief on Mrs. Quently's face as she returned to her chair. Mrs. Quently looked at Matt and said that two investigators from the Homicide Unit were waiting outside to talk to him, and that she would give him a few minutes between tests to meet with them.

Matt finished the examination with a little more than ten minutes left. He closed the examination book, placed the answer sheet on top of it and then the pencils of top of that. He sat patiently in the silent classroom until the time completely expired at which point Mrs. Quently walked over to his desk and picked up the materials that were laying on it.

She told Matt that he had ten minutes for a break or to speak with the investigators wondering to herself why detectives wanted to talk to a police applicant.

Matt walked out into the reception area where the two detectives were standing by a drink vending machine. They introduced themselves as Sergeant Dave Weeman and Specialist Rudy Grenko from the Cincinnati Police Homicide Section. Weeman looked to be in his late forties with graying hair and a ruddy complexion while Grenko looked to be in his mid-thirties with a beer belly and auburn hair that looked like it had been cut at a Barber college by a student.

Weeman told Matt that the two detectives would like to buy him lunch and talk about what he had seen the previous night and that they would pick him up after his physical examination was complete.

Matt returned to the classroom seeing the quizzical look on Mrs. Quently's face and, without saying a word, returned to his seat indicating that he was ready to complete the second phase of the test.

Mrs. Quently read the instructions for the second phase of the examination. She placed another booklet on the desk in front of him and ordered him not to touch it until told to do so. Matt would have ten minutes to read and digest the information contained in the booklet and it would then be removed and replaced by another booklet containing the questions for the test. He would also get a second answer sheet to choose the correct answer for each question and would have a twenty minute time limit. She again asked Matt if he had any questions before the test began. When he replied he did not, she told him to open the book.

When Matt opened the book it contained the pictures and descriptions of four people as well as their criminal records and what they were currently wanted for by the police. Matt made sure to commit to memory the hair color and facial hair on the three males and searched the pictures for identifying factors such as tattoos and/or scars. The fourth picture was of a female who had a butch haircut and a large tattoo on the right side of her neck.

When the ten minutes was over, Mrs. Quently walked over to the desk and scooped up the booklet, replacing it with two new pencils, a test booklet and an answer sheet. Matt completed the test portion in less than fifteen minutes and walked up to the desk where Mrs. Quently was seated placing the materials on the desk. Mrs. Quently picked up all of the test materials and placed them in a folder marked "Miles, M. W.". She then left without wishing him success or even saying good bye.

Matt's next stop was the medical doctor contracted by the City to perform applicant physicals. It was about five miles from the Police Academy in what appeared to be a medical complex near the campus of the University of Cincinnati.

When he approached the reception desk Matt was greeted by an early twenties young woman who actually had a smile on her face and some personality. She greeted him warmly when he told her he was there for a police applicant physical examination. She handed him a stack of forms that he needed to fill out prior to being seen by the doctor, provided him with a pen and told him to check back with her if he had any questions.

The forms asked questions about every possible ailment, many of which Matt had never even heard of. When he was finished he returned the clipboard to the woman at the desk who then took him down a hallway and into an empty treatment room. The woman said a nurse would be in shortly to see him.

The nurse was a very pretty woman in her forties who told Matt that she would need to get two blood samples which would then be tested for drug use and STDs. She would also be taking his blood pressure and measuring his height, weight and body mass. She instructed him to strip down to his t-shirt and underwear for her. Matt was embarrassed when he told her that he did not, as a rule wear undergarments, and asked her how she wanted to deal with this issue. The nurse seemed to enjoy his blushing and asked if Matt would rather have her go get a male nurse for this. Matt told the woman that he just wanted to get it completed and stripped naked for her.

The nurse began by taking his blood pressure which was well within normal range and then measured him a six feet exactly and his weight at two hundred and five pounds. She smiled when she checked his body fat and found it to be just over six percent. She asked Matt if he had played athletics and he told her that he enjoyed surfing since he was from the west coast. The nurse took two vials of blood and sealed them with tape placing her initials on the top of each of the vials to keep them from being tampered with. The nurse told Matt to put his clothes back on and the Doctor would be in to see him shortly. Matt took notice of the glint in the nurse's eye when she looked at his manhood,

It took what seemed to be an inordinate amount of time for the Doctor to finally come into the room. The interview was really short and the doctor did not seem to be very interested in the examination. He told Matt that the results of the examination would be forwarded to the Civil Service Commission and that he could request, in writing, a copy of those results.

Matt walked back toward the reception area and immediately saw the two detectives in the waiting room. He walked out to meet them where they shook hands and the Sergeant said it was time to eat.

Matt was taken to a restaurant called Frisch's which claimed to be the home of the Big Boy sandwich. Having been to Kip's on the west coast, Matt felt comfortable ordering the double-decker hamburger off the menu. He was truly surprised to see tartar sauce and pickles on the sandwich and the two detectives just laughed and said that all out of towners were surprised to see that.

As they were eating the Sergeant asked Matt to recall as much as possible about what he seen in the alley. Matt closed his eyes and tried to visualize everything he saw and heard. He told the detectives he was walking back to the hotel when he heard what sounded like soft moans coming from an alley off to his right. As soon as he looked down the alley he saw a male running in the opposite direction of him and he never did see the face of the male. He also saw something laying in the middle of the alley and that is when he called the police on his cell phone. He told them he never approached whatever was in the alley because, if it was a crime scene, he did not want to disturb it, but that it did not occur to him that it might be a person laying in the alley. He only found out that it was a woman when the first officers entered the alley with their flashlights.

The younger detective told Matt that the woman was a twenty year old waitress who had just gotten off of work. She died of stab wounds and was not wearing any underwear and wanted to know if Matt had seen anything in the suspect's hands like a knife or maybe her underwear. Matt again closed his eyes and saw the man running away but could not distinguish anything being in either of the man's hands.

The Sergeant asked Matt if he saw anything that identified the race of the person running and Matt said he did not. The detectives next wanted to know how Matt could possibly know that the suspect was wearing sneakers if he could not tell the race or age of him. Matt told them he did not hear the sounds of the shoe soles hitting the pavement which is what led him to that conclusion.

The younger detective told Matt that they were able to lift shoeprints in the area where Matt saw the guy running and that they appeared to be made by running shoes of some sort. He thanked Matt for that information and they wrapped up lunch because Matt still had the physical agility and run yet to do. The detectives told Matt they would send a car to his hotel about five o'clock to take him to the Criminal Investigation Section office to give a written statement.

When they dropped him back at his car, both detectives wished him well In becoming a Cincinnati cop.

***

Matt arrived back at Spinney Field with just enough time to change into his workout clothes for the afternoon testing.

He was met by two of the Police Academy instructors who also happened to be brothers. Tim and Tom Hatterfeld joined the police department within a year of each and been both assigned to the

Training Division for the past two years. Both brothers greeted Matt warmly and told him that they wanted him to succeed. They said they had also heard about his first night in Cincinnati and told him that he saw the first homicide of the year in the downtown area.

Matt was given fifteen minutes to loosen up and do whatever warm-up exercises he chose. Matt used the same routine he always did whenever he went surfing because it loosened the leg and back muscles for him. Tim retrieved a police gun belt that had pieces of block to simulate the weight of a gun and a portable radio and told Matt he would be wearing it throughout the tests.

Matt was then taken to the obstacle course where Tom lost the coin toss with his brother and had to run the demonstration. Matt would have ninety seconds to complete the obstacle course which consisted of a short run down a track, climbing through a window, running a short distance, climbing an eight foot wall, running another short distance and then ringing a bell. Tom ran the course while Tim kept the time. It took Tom sixty-seven seconds.

Tom told Matt the time would start on the blowing of the whistle and end when Matt rang the bell. He asked Matt if he had any questions. When Matt said he did not, Tom blew the whistle. The window was something that Matt had never experienced but he had watched Tom grab the top of the window and slide his body through so that is what Matt did as well. He was definitely out of breath as he rang the bell to end the test. His time was eighty-four seconds.

The next exercise involved the dragging of a one hundred fifty pound dummy up three steps, across a wood plank for fifty feet and then down a set of three steps. There was no time limit on this test, but once it started, Matt was told that he was not permitted to stop until he completed the down steps. This time Tim did the demonstration and made it look easy, so Matt was comfortable when it was his turn. He completed the exercise easily and was not even winded.

Matt was asked if he wanted to get water or re-stretch prior to the next phase which consisted of a one and one half mile run immediately followed by push-ups, sit-ups and pull-ups. Matt declined the offer and wanted to get through this phase of the testing.

Matt would have twelve minutes to complete the run and would be told his time after lap three. Cincinnati had just installed a synthetic rubber running surface on the quarter mile track in order to reduce shin splint and pulled muscle injuries. Matt would be taken to the inside of the running track where he would be required to do thirty sit-ups, thirty push-ups and twelve pull-ups, each with a one minute time limit.

As Matt walked to the starting line Tom advised him to set a comfortable pace in his first three of the six laps and that his time at end of those laps could be adjusted either way to get him under the time limit. Tim also suggested that Matt save some energy so that he would be able to sprint the last lap and get it done. Matt really appreciated the advice of both of the brothers.

Matt stood at the starting line and was asked if he was ready. Tim blew the whistle and the clock began. After completing half the run, Matt was surprised to hear that he was almost a full minute behind where he thought he was and needed to pick up the pace. When he crossed the starting line for his final lap, Matt remembered the advice and decided to wind-sprint the final lap. He crossed the finish line in eleven minutes and forty-two seconds.

Matt was working to control his breathing as they walked to the area where the chin up bar was located. He was told to do the sit-ups first, then the push-ups and then the pull-ups last. Both Tim and Tom were smiling when they told him he had passed the tests. They wished him well as they escorted him back to his car.

Matt drove slowly back to the hotel happy in what he had accomplished to this point. He needed to call his parents and give them the good news. He got back to his room but really wanted a shower before calling his parents.

He was relaxing on the bed after the refreshing shower when he picked up the phone to call mom and dad. He had already decided to leave out the details of his first night in Cincinnati because he did not want them to be alarmed. He told his mom about each of the phases of the testing and she would then relay it to his father. Mom said she has never been more pleased with her son than she was at that moment.

It was almost five o'clock when his room phone rang. It was a male voice who identified himself as Police Specialist Andrew Bartold and that he would take Matt to the Investigation Section for his statement, but wanted Matt to return to the alley and walk through what had happened. The alley looked much different during daylight and Matt could see that the alley was squeezed between two large structures and had been used by drug addicts because there were used needles laying on the ground. Matt showed Bartold the direction Matt had come from and what his position was when he heard the commotion that caught his attention.

On the way to the office, Matt asked Bartold, since he was not much older than Matt, where to go to relax on his last night in Cincy. Bartold told Matt that there was a zone just north of downtown with microbreweries that drew a fairly young and enthusiastic crowd. Bartold told Matt to leave his rental car at the hotel and take a cab to and from. Bartold said the bars all hired off-duty cops to work security and that, should a problem occur, Matt should tell the cop that he is in town for the Police test.

Matt was escorted into the Criminal Investigation Section and the area looked
just like he had seen on television. There were desks everywhere and cops sitting at them talking on their phone or working at the computer. Bartold led him back to an interview room and asked if it was okay for the interview to be videotaped for evidence. Bartold walked through the same things Matt had told the detectives twice before. After they were done, Specialist Bartold returned Matt to his hotel and wished him well.

Matt clicked on the television and the local news. The lead story was about a twenty year old woman who had been murdered in an alley between Main and Walnut Street late last night. The anchor told viewers that reporter Rich Jakki was live at the scene with the story. A survey of viewers of the news conducted by a reputable group had determined that live shots, even when there was no action taking place, kept their interest more than just reporting a story. Jakki, wearing his signature cowboy hat, was standing in almost the exact spot that Matt had been the night before. The camera was showing an empty alley where the crime scene tape had already been taken down and the crime scene people and the cops were long gone.

Jakki told viewers that twenty year old JoAnn Wordly of Western Hills left her job as a waitress just after eleven o'clock and was found in an alley dead of stab wounds. Jakki said police were being very tight-lipped about a witness who saw a man running out of the alley and that police were awaiting a report from the Coroner as to whether the twenty year old had been sexually assaulted prior to being killed. Jakki said police had found Wordly's car parked at a parking meter on Third Street and they believed she was walking toward her car when the incident occurred. Jakki ended the story the way all reporters do by saying, "Live from the scene, this is Rich Jakke, Local 12 News."

Matt lay on the bed somewhat remorseful that he had not gone into the alley to help the young woman, even though it probably would have not changed the outcome. He felt that a real police officer would have gone after the guy he saw running and began wondering to himself if he really wanted to be a cop after all.

It was time to decide his actions for the evening. It had been a long day of physical activity and the fact that he had not slept well caused him to rethink whether to check out the nightlife in Cincinnati on this trip. Matt decided on a nice relaxing dinner and just lounge in front of the television so that he would be rested for tomorrow's grueling tests.

Matt fell asleep watching an episode of CSI.

CHAPTER THREE

Matt awoke prior to the wake-up call from the front desk. He actually felt pretty relaxed as he got up to take his shower and pack his bags for the trip home. He had to jump out of the shower to answer the call from the front desk and was pissed that he had not remembered to cancel it.

Once again, his mother had perfectly color coordinated his outfit for the second day. She had packed gray dress slacks, an off-white short sleeve shirt, a light blue conservative tie, and a royal blue blazer. Matt slowly packed his belongings getting ready to check out of the hotel and decided on the breakfast bar in the hotel before starting his day.

His polygraph test would be conducted at C.I.S. headquarters that is a place he had already been. He arrived at the building ten minutes early and told the policeman sitting at the desk that he was scheduled for a polygraph. The desk man picked up the phone and told whoever was on the other end of the line that his eight o'clock was waiting.

Specialist Dan Agostic had just over thirty years on the job. His wife told him that the day after he retired that she would file for divorce because he exhibited the same personality at home as he did at work. Agostic was wearing a suit that looked like he had slept in it and had a face that only a mother could love. He did not like his job, even though it was Monday through Friday with all holidays off. He did not like interacting with people. Most of all, he did not like anything about his miserable existence. Agostic relished the fact that he was able to elicit information from police applicants that got them eliminated and had little skeletons on the wall for each applicant he was able to break. Agostc treated police applicants exactly the same as he did criminal suspects, and prided himself on the fact that he had no friends and really did not want any.

Matt was standing at the desk when Agostic walked up. Without saying a word, Agostic motioned for Matt to follow him down the hall. Matt sized up the man who would be administering the lie detector test and concluded that this was not going to be a fun experience. Agostic led Matt into a room that perfectly mirrored the overweight and disheveled cop's personality. The walls were a drab off-white color and there was a desk with a computer, a blank legal pad, a pen and a phone on it. There were no pictures on the wall or anything that would personalize the area. There was a door in the back left corner and a glass window showing another drab room with a table, two chairs and a box of some kind on the table.

Agostic pointed toward the only other chair in the room indicating that Matt should sit down. Matt sat in the chair and listened as the operator introduced himself and told Matt that he would asking a series of questions that the morons in the Police Chief's office thought were important for any police applicant and that all of the questions on the polygraph would be answered with a "no" by Matt.

He went on to say that there would be no ambiguous questions on the machine because both he and Matt would find a common ground where Matt was comfortable answering no to.

Agostic reached into the top right hand drawer of the desk and pulled out a stack of papers. Matt was beginning to get very nervous at this point since the operator had done nothing to make him feel comfortable. Matt was asked about whether he had ever stolen anything valued at more than five cents and the amount kept rising until they agreed he had never stolen anything valued at more than twenty-five dollars. The interview portion took just over an hour to complete at which time Agostic stood up and motioned Matt into the adjoining room.

Matt sat down in the single chair other than the one behind the desk and felt the cold emanating from the air conditioning in the room that was almost as uncomfortable as was the décor of the room itself.

Agostic wrapped a blood pressure cup tightly to Matt's right arm and then wrapped a rubber coated wire around Matt's chest. The last thing he did was slide a cover over Matt's baby finger on his right hand. Matt took notice that he was facing away from the desk and could not see the box located on top of the desk or the operator. Matt was told to look straight forward at all times during the test and to just relax and give truthful answers.

The first question asked was whether Matt had been truthful in the answers he put on the application form with the City and then there were many questions that the two had agreed on in the interview. The lie detector test was over in less than fifteen minutes.

Without saying a word Specialist Agostic removed the wires that had been connected to Matt and escorted him back to the front desk of C.I.S. Matt had hoped that some cue would be provided as to how he did on the test, but the old guy gave him no indication. In fact, Agostic had not even said good bye or wished him well. Matt thought to himself that this man has no class at all.

Agostic walked back to his office angry that he had not been able to break or even rattle this kid who apparently had led a really boring life. He would not be able to provide much that would get this kid scrubbed from the applicant list. His job was getting less fun with each passing day.

Matt walked back to his car to look at the directions to get to the office of the police psychologist. He tried not to reflect on what had just occurred because he would have ample time on the flight. He easily found the office that was also near the University campus. He looked at the flowing campus of the University of Cincinnati and was impressed by how easily people seemed to move around and the relaxed atmosphere it presented.

Matt walked up to the receptionist who offered a genuine smile as he told her about his appointment for the police applicant testing. She chatted briefly asking him if he was a homegrown Cincinnatian. When he told her that he flew in from Los Angeles for the tests, she laughed and told him she should have caught that by his tan.

She led him to a room equipped with one desk and one chair and explained that he would be administered the Minnesota Multiphasic Personality Inventory test. She explained that there are no right or wrong answers to the test and to just answer them honestly. There would be a total of five hundred and fifty-six questions and that he was to answer all of them. When he told her he had no questions about the process, she placed a test booklet, a pencil and an answer sheet on the desk in front of him and quietly closed the door. Matt had heard of the MMPI from his psychology classes at UCLA and knew that it measured personality structure and psychopathology.

He methodically read each question and answered each one the best that he could. Matt took note that some of the questions appeared to be the same as earlier questions, just worded differently.

When he was done answering all the questions, he took the booklet and answer sheet back to the reception desk where the woman told him he would have a little over an hour to grab lunch before the doctor would see him. She suggested a little hole in the wall on McMillian Street called the Bearcat Lounge and said it drew a college age crowd, had great sandwiches and was within walking distance. Matt thanked the woman and wandered off for his lunch.

As Matt walked down Taft Road, named after William Howard Taft who was a President of the United States and a native of Cincinnati, he was admiring the architecture of the college buildings. Matt knew Cincinnati was well known for its basketball program and that one of its former football coaches was now coaching the storied program at Notre Dame, but didn't know much else. He leisurely ate his sandwich and slowly walked back for the final leg of his testing.

The psychologist for the Cincinnati Police Department was an independent contractor who had chosen to specialize in law enforcement officers. He had well over twenty years experience in dealing with officers who had been involved in police shootings and other traumatic events. He was tasked with determining whether working cops and wannabe cops were fit for duty. The doctor had seen firsthand the effect that a single incident had on people who chose law enforcement as a career.

The doctor walked out into the waiting wearing an open collar short sleeve shirt and slacks. Matt took notice that the doctor looked relaxed and that had a calming effect. The doctor took Matt into a room that was full of pastel colors and pictures on the walls. There were two comfortable chairs facing each other.

The doctor began the interview by telling Matt that this would be an informal conversation in an attempt to get to know Matt and find out what kind of person Matt really is. The first question that the doctor asked Matt was about Matt's first experience in Cincinnati, which put Matt in a bit of a quandary since he did not know whether or not to mention the fact that he witnessed a murder. Matt decided not to mention that and focused on the sights and sounds that he had experienced as well as the different foods that he had tasted.

When the doctor asked specifically about the murder, Matt was astonished. The doctor simply laughed and said that he received information about applicants from the Police Department prior to their scheduled interview on a regular basis. Matt decided to confide in the doctor that he felt some remorse about not taking any action other than calling the police and providing information as he recalled it. The doctor laughed again and told Matt that the Police Academy teaches men and women how and when to react to certain situations and that the report that he received from the Police Department indicated Matt had done everything right.

The one hour interview felt to Matt like it had lasted only about ten minutes. The doctor wished Matt a safe trip back to Los Angeles and the best success in his career search. Matt left the office feeling comfortable about how he had been treated and was ready for the final phase.

The last portion of the testing would be conducted at the main police headquarters on Ezzard Charles Drive. Matt would later learn that Ezzard Charles was an Olympic boxer from Cincinnati. Matt had been told to park in the employee lot which is located in the rear of the police building. He arrived just as the shifts were changing so the parking lot was active with cops in uniform entering and leaving. Matt walked around to the front of the oblong three story building to the desk which was protected by bullet proof glass. He was escorted by a uniformed police officer to the third floor and then directed into a conference room where there was one chair in the center of the room and four people seated behind a long table. Three of the four were wearing police uniforms and the fourth was a woman in civilian clothes. He sat quietly in his chair as each introduced themselves to him. There was one Assistant Chief of Police, one Captain, one

Sergeant and the only female who was from the Cincinnati Civil Service Commission.

The board seemed a bit concerned that Matt had no employment history whatsoever, but Matt seamlessly explained it by telling the members although his parents were not rich by any means, that they wanted him to be able to focus totally on his education. He told the members that he had done some yard work for neighbors to pick up extra spending money as a teenager, but had no conventional work history.

The interview lasted less than thirty minutes and the board members told him that a decision would be made in four to six weeks and that he would be notified by mail. Matt was unsure how he fared with the questions that were asked as he walked toward the parking lot, Matt felt that overall he had done well. He drove leisurely back into Kentucky taking in the scenery to catch his plane home.

CHAPTER FOUR

As the plane reached its altitude and the seats could be pushed back, Matt relaxed and tried to reflect on what had occurred over the past two days. He felt that no matter the outcome of employment that he had matured since arriving in Cincinnati and his priorities were completely different than when he arrived.

Matt closed his eyes to mentally reenact what he had done well and what areas needed improvement. He woke up when the pilot announced that the plane was approaching Los Angeles, California and that it was eight-ten pm and ninety-one degrees in the west coast city of angels.

Matt went directly to the baggage area before calling his parents to pick him up. When no one answered his home phone number he called his father's cell phone only to find that his parents were already at LAX and were looking for him. When his parents finally located him in the baggage area, Matt's mother noticed that there was something different about her son than when he left for Cincinnati. Matt had a new persona and a glow about him that indicated a new air of maturity she had never seen before.

On the ride home Matt talked about seeing the campus of the University of Cincinnati and how different it was from UCLA. He talked about the historic architecture and the clean downtown. His parents laughed when he told them about the shock of landing at an airport that was in Kentucky. Matt told his parents that he would take them through his experiences at breakfast the next morning and that he wanted to take this night to just relax and have a beer or two near the campus.

Matt drove his Mustang to a local bar that he had frequented during his college life. He sat down on a stool and admired the bartender who appeared to be in her mid-twenties with long brown hair. When the bartender came for his order he flashed a nice smile and asked for a light draft beer. The bartender smiled back and introduced herself as Margot. Matt was sitting on the stool watching Margot's every move as she flowed from one end of the bar to the other making drinks and small talk with the patrons. Margot finally got back to him and asked whether he just wanted to ogle her all night or was he interested in more. Matt checked out her snug fitting pale blue blouse and her tight skirt and told her he was interested in much more. Margot told him that her shift ended at ten thirty if he would to wait around. He ordered another beer and sipped on it slowly.

Matt followed Margot out into the parking lot where she told him to follow her to her place which was just on the other side of the campus of UCLA. He walked back to his car and drove to her and then followed her to her place. When they walked into the apartment Matt noticed that the décor was low key and pleasant with just a couch, a chair, two end tables with lamps, a small table in front of the couch and a television in the living room. The dining room had a small table and three chairs and the kitchen looked big enough for one person to be in at a time. Margot went to the refrigerator and got out two bottles of beer, opening them and handing one to Matt. Matt had dropped the blazer and the tie, but was still wearing the shirt and pants that he wore to the interview in Cincinnati.

Margot took her beer and walked toward a doorway in the back of the apartment and Matt assumed she wanted him to follow. The doorway led to a bedroom which had an expansive bed, a dresser and one end table. Margot was already taking off her blouse and bra to expose her firm 36c breasts. Matt felt his manhood react to this marvelous woman's body. She placed her arms around Matt's neck and he could feel the cold of the beer bottle on the back of his shoulder. Margot dropped her left hand to feel his crotch and giggled at the fact that he had an erection. Margot placed her bottle of beer on the table and moved to take off Matt's shirt. She licked on his nipples making him twitch and lightly moan. He could see that her eyes were enjoying his toned upper torso.

Margot turned around and suggested to Matt that he unzip her skirt and, when it hit the floor he was surprised that she was not wearing any panties. She turned and released the clip on Matt's pants and then unzipped them sliding them slowly down his legs and waiting for him to lift each foot to get his pants off. By now Matt was throbbing and he could tell that Margot was enjoying every moment of teasing him. She next removed his underwear and they fell softly onto the floor.

Margot reached under her bed to retrieve a plastic sheet that looked like a large diaper which she placed strategically onto the bed. Margot then told Matt to lay down on his back on the sheet. Matt blushed as he had to tell her that he did not have any protection, but she only giggled again and opened the drawer on the end table that had condoms and what looked like different dildos in it. Matt decided that he needed to take control of this situation, so he told her that she would have to put it on him. She slowly unwrapped the condom and tantalizingly unrolled it down his throbbing erection, then mounted him until he was all the way inside her.

The next thing Margot did was unexpected as she leaned over to the end table and turned the radio on so the music was blaring in Matt's ear. As she began moving slowly up and down on him, her soft moans became louder and louder and he understood that the music was intended to drown out her screams of ecstasy. When they were done the sheet below was soaking wet from her juices and they were both worn out.

They got out of the bed and Margot folded the soaked sheet and tossed it in a hamper. They finished their beer and decided to shower together and he left for home with a smile the size of California. Margot told Matt that the next time she might invite a girlfriend for a little three way action.

Halfway home Matt remembered that he had not gotten Margot's telephone number, but he knew where and when she worked and he would make it a point to frequent that bar more often.

***

Matt woke up after what had been his most relaxing sleep ever. He wandered down the stairs to the kitchen where his mother and father were both sitting drinking their coffee. As his mother made him a special breakfast of French toast stuffed with custard, he took them step-by-step through his testing experience in Cincinnati. He saved the part about going to see the new riverfront park in Cincinnati and then witnessing the murder until the very last thing. His father asked if he felt scared during the incident and, after thinking for a few seconds, Matt said he really did not have time to be in fear because it was all over so quickly. Matt told his parents he really liked the detectives that talked to him and took his statement. He also told them that he had told the psychologist that he felt remorse over not doing more, but that the doctor said he did everything right.

After breakfast, Matt decided to grab his surf board and head out to the beach for the afternoon sun. It was going to be a beautiful day along the Los Angeles coast line and Matt felt good about the way his life was turning out. The sand would be warm under his feet and the ocean would be cold and blue. If he landed the job in Cincinnati that would be what he would miss most. Matt would just have to wait for Cincinnati to make a decision as he was finally ready to start the next phase of his life.

Matt was at the door every day for the next two weeks to meet the postman and see if the letter from Cincinnati had arrived. His parents had told him that he did not need to make any other applications until he got an answer from the City. The suspense was killing him.

***

Back in Cincinnati, Sergeant Dave Weeman and Specialist Rudy Grenko had been assigned to investigate the homicide of JoAnn Wordly and were having a difficult time putting together what had happened. The Coroner's report said that Wordly died from two stab wounds to the left side of her body. The two investigators determined that Wordly left her waitress job shortly before eleven o'clock and was walking south on Main Street toward Third Street where her car was parked at a parking meter. If a Sergeant at the scene had not ordered a uniform officer to run license plate checks on all the vehicles parked in the area around Fourth and Main, her car might not have been located for days, weeks or even months. Cincinnati restricts rush hour parking in the morning and afternoon on weekdays and the car would have been towed to the Impounding Lot and just sat there.

A surveillance camera across the street showed video of the alley from Walnut Street and confirmed the statement of the witness as to his whereabouts but did not show any of the activity in the alley itself. The two investigators re-traced the path that Wordly would have likely taken to see if they could find any other cameras that might have captured the victim or her attacker. They located a camera outside of an office building at Fifth and Walnut that has twenty-four hour security, but when they went inside to the Security Office they were told that the view they needed was only live and not recorded. They made a note to themselves to return and talk to the guard who was on duty as he might recall a pretty woman walking alone at eleven pm.

Weeman and Grenko had talked to all of the night shift employees at the restaurant and learned that Wordly had a boyfriend, although no one knew his name or had ever seen him. The investigators were told that Wordly lived with her grandmother on the west side of town and that the boyfriend could be living there also. Weeman and

Grenko drove to the address at 1121 Mustang Drive. They were walking around the outside of the house when a woman who appeared to be in her late sixties came out of the house next door and yelled at them to get away from the house. When they identified themselves as police officers the woman told the officers that she had not seen any movement in or around the house since the day of JoAnn's death. She had seen JoAnn get into her car about two o'clock that afternoon which was the normal time she left for work. The woman stated that she had concern because she had not seen JoAnn's grandmother either and wondered if she was okay.

The investigators asked about a man possibly living in the house as well. The woman told them she had seen a man coming and going from the house but that she did not know his name or the relationship he had with the family. She described him as being about Grenko's height which was five feet ten inches, having a slim build and dark wavy hair. Weeman gave the woman his business card and told her to call him if anyone came around the house.

The investigators walked around Wordly's house and knocked on all the exterior doors and checked to make sure they were locked. There was no car in the one car garage. They looked in all the windows and saw no sign of any activity in the house and decided that they would need to go to a Judge and obtain a search warrant to get inside the house and search any possible evidence of foul play with the grandmother.

Weeman used his portable radio to get a uniform car to sit on the house while the two investigators drew up the search warrant and presented it to a Judge. They drove back to the C.I.S. office where there were search warrants on the computer that they only needed to plug in the address to be searched and a few facts to justify the issuance of the warrant. They drove down to the courthouse and found a Judge who signed it without even reading what it said.

With the warrant in hand and a couple of crime scene technicians, the investigators forced open the rear door and went inside the house. It was, like most in the neighborhood, built in the forties or fifties and was a small house having two floors and a basement. They started what it called a grid search that sections off each area to assure that nothing is missed.

The basement looked like it had not been used in many years, having just a few tools and a washer and dryer. There were no clothes in either the washer or the dryer. The first floor consisted of a living room with older furniture, a kitchen, a dining room and one bathroom. Everything in the house so far showed no indication of any male living there. There were no ashtrays which told investigators that none of the occupants smoked. There were no dishes in the sink or any indication that the stove had been recently used. There was mail in the mailbox and investigators made a note to check with the letter carrier at the earliest opportunity to determine when the last time him or her saw the occupants.

While one crime scene tech was taking photos of the whole house, the other was using fingerprint powder to attempt to lift prints off of areas likely to have been recently used. The hope was that one or more of the prints would lead to identifying the mysterious boyfriend of JoAnn Wordly.

Investigators moved up the steps to the second floor of the house. When they reached the top step they found a hallway which ran to the right and left. The left side of the hallway led to a master bedroom with its own bathroom. The bed was neatly made and the room was clean and undisturbed. In the closet the investigators saw woman's clothing in a size four hanging neatly side by side. The shoes on the floor of the closet indicated a small statured woman. The bathroom was clean and had a few feminine products on the sink and the toilet seat was down, an indication that it was only used by a female. The investigators placed the toothbrush in an evidence container to be sent to the lab for possible DNA.

The last stop in the house was the bedroom at the other end of the hall. The bed in this room was neatly made as well and there were pictures of what appeared to be a high school graduation of JoAnn. There was a laptop computer in the room which the crime scene techs placed in a bag to be analyzed. The closet and the house showed no evidence that a male had spent a significant amount of time there and the investigators retrieved the only toothbrush in the bathroom to match against JoAnn's DNA. They also bagged the hairbrushes found in the house as well.

The investigators wrote all of the items removed on an inventory sheet that was attached to the search warrant and left a copy on the dining room table for whoever came home to find along with a business card of Sergeant Grenko which had the handwritten message "PLEASE CALL!"

The investigators decided to end their workday by delivering the materials taken from the house directly to the police property room rather than taking the items back to the office and adding a layer to the chain of custody.

The investigators started their morning with the Homicide Unit briefing where all of the investigators report to the Homicide Lieutenant their progress on the case they are assigned. Sergeant Grenko really did not want to announce that they were nowhere with the investigation into the death of JoAnn Wordly, but that was the reality. He did want the thoughts of the other investigators that no one had seen or heard from the grandmother either. Grenko announced that he and Weeman would be going to the high school that Wordly graduated from to see if they could identify any friends or former teachers who might know who the unidentified boyfriend might be. Another detective not assigned to this case made the suggestion to check the local colleges to see if Wordly was taking classes somewhere.

***

Grenko and Weeman drove to Western Hills High School and went directly to the Principal's Office to pull the records for JoAnn. The school records showed that she excelled in academics in her time at the school and had no disciplinary issues. The Principal suggested the investigators speak with Mrs. Bernice Waterson, the school's guidance counselor who had been with the School for over twenty years.

The investigators went to the Guidance Office just down the hall from the main office and introduced themselves to Mrs. Waterson. When Specialist Weeman asked Mrs. Waterson about JoAnn Wordly the counsellor's face lit up and she said she knew the young lady well from her days at West Hi. Mrs. Waterson told the investigators that JoAnn's grandmother became her legal guardian when JoAnn was fifteen because her parents were killed in a car crash. JoAnn had received a large settlement from the insurance company that covered the driver of the other car who was drunk at the wheel. The driver was convicted of Vehicular Manslaughter and was serving a sentence in prison.

Sergeant Grenko asked if Mrs. Waterson knew any of JoAnn's friends, especially a potential boyfriend. Mrs. Waterson found a yearbook and began looking for pictures of JoAnn and found one of her at a football game with another girl Mrs. Waterson believed was Jennifer Hok. She checked the computer and found a home address of Jennifer's parents and told the investigators that the loss of JoAnn was a shame because she was a classy young lady. The investigators thanked her and returned to the office.

Ownership of the house on Mustang was traced to a woman named Danise Davis. They then took that information and cross checked it with Motor Vehicle records which showed Mrs. Davis owned a 2008 Ford Taurus with Ohio license plates 2079CPD. There was no vehicle in the garage, but no one had checked to see what was parked on the street. The investigators returned to the house and found the vehicle parked across the street from the residence which made them more suspicious as to the whereabouts of Danise Davis.

They had already talked to one neighbor, so they decided to canvas the neighborhood to see if anyone knew the whereabouts of Davis or had more information on the male. Since it was a work day, most were not home and they would have to try again in the evening hours.

CHAPTER FIVE

Matt was at home checking the mail every day in the hope of hearing back from Cincinnati as almost two weeks had passed since his tests were completed. Matt had spoken to his parents about seeking summer employment while he was waiting for an answer, but they told him that they would take care of his expenses for a while longer.

Not a day had gone by that Matt did not think about what he saw in that alley in Cincinnati. He looked through his wallet and found the business card of the investigator that he gave the statement to and thought about calling him to see if there were any leads in the case. He picked up the phone and dialed the number of Specialist Bartold, who just happened to be at his desk. Bartold told Matt that the investigation was not assigned to him but the two investigators who were working the case were not having much luck so far. Bartold asked Matt if he had remembered any additional details that might help, but Matt said he did not. Bartold then asked if Matt had heard anything on his status with Civil Service and Matt just sighed into the phone and said he was awaiting the letter. Bartold told Matt that if he remembered anything that might help the investigators to call Sgt. Grenko and gave him the direct line number to the Sgt.'s desk. Bartold wished him luck and hung up.

Matt felt really frustrated that he was unable to offer more information about the crime he had witnessed then he remembered an episode of NCIS where a hypnotist was used to help an agent remember what he had seen. Matt picked up the phone and called the LA County Sheriff's Office and asked for the Homicide Division. This was Corporal Gary Berry's day at the desk and Matt explained that he had been in Cincinnati, Ohio for a police job and witnessed a murder. Matt was wondering if LASO had a hypnotist that they used and the Corporal could verify his story with Cincinnati PD. Cpl. Berry's day to this point had been really boring and he truly believed that he had one more whack-job on the phone. But something deep inside him told him to check out the caller's story and so he asked Matt for a number to call him back after he checked some things out.

Berry contacted Cincinnati Police and was told that the story was legitimate. He then called a friend who contracted with the LASO for hypnosis and asked if the doctor would be willing to get involved in an Ohio case. The doctor was reluctant at first, but he too had a gut instinct that made him accept. The doctor told Cpl. Berry that he would need the sketch of the crime scene and one photo showing it as well. Cpl. Berry called Cincinnati Homicide back and within ten minutes Cincinnati had sent the requested documents to Berry's inbox.

Matt reached into his right hand pocket to retrieve his ringing cell phone and saw that the screen only said "private number." He was surprised when the caller told him he was Cpl. Berry of the LA County Sheriff and that the doctor would like to see him. Cpl. Berry gave Matt a number to call to make the appointment.

***

When Sgt. Grenko arrived for work, he saw the message light on his phone flashing. It was a call from the Regional Electronic Computer Intelligence Unit of the Hamilton County Sheriff's Department saying that they had analyzed the computer taken from the home of JoAnn Wordly. Grenko called the Unit and asked for Det. Dave Ausdenmire who was a Cincinnati cop assigned to the Task Force. Ausdenmire said that Wordly had an electronic diary she kept on her computer and that the task force had printed him a copy to read over. Ausdenmire also said that analysts were able to identify both her Facebook and Twitter accounts, but that the only pictures posted were of her.

Since Cincinnati had experienced two more homicides since Wordly's death, the two investigators would be assigned the next one and needed to get this case moving quickly.

Grenko and Weeman drove over to the Justice Center where the R.E.C.I. Unit was located and picked up the printouts of the diary, Facebook page, and Twitter account. They drove to a Frisch's and sat in a booth with their coffee looking over the last days of JoAnn's diary. She identified a male as being a boyfriend and listed his name only as Willie. She described him as being older than her but that he treated her as a princess and that their sex together was always an enjoyable experience.

Grenko and Weeman returned to the office and commandeered a conference room where they spread out everything they had to this point and two blank legal pads to make notes. They also had the coroner's autopsy report which had just arrived. The cause of death was easy, but the coroner had to wait on the toxicology report which included a swab taken from the vaginal cavity which showed that JoAnn had vaginal sex within the twenty four hour period prior to her death. DNA had been recovered but there was no match in the national C.O.D.I.S. database. There was no sign of rape or any force used so it was unlikely that she had been raped in the alley.

Another report that neither investigator had seen showed that an insurance company had settled with the estate of JoAnn's parents in the amount of one million two hundred thousand dollars. The trustee for the estate, since JoAnn would have been only fifteen at the time, was her grandmother who had not been seen either.

Weeman made a note to check the bank records of the trust to see if there had been any recent withdrawals. This case was simply not going to be easy to solve.

CHAPTER SIX

Matt walked up to the door with a sign that said Dr. Michael No, M.D. He had no idea what he would find on the other side of the door and there was both anticipation and fear in his eyes when he went to the check-in desk. The nurse gave him a form to fill out and a profile of the doctor for him to read. Dr. No had completed his medical training in the Philippines and was Board certified in clinical and forensic hypnotherapy from Johns Hopkins University.

The doctor opened the inner door and smiled at Matt, inviting him back to a hallway and into a treatment room. The room itself was relaxing in that it had pictures of an expansive sand beach and a beautiful waterway and the room had lounge chairs that were plush, deep and large.

Matt slid into the chair and the two exchanged small talk for a couple of minutes. No asked Matt what he knew about hypnosis and Matt replied little to nothing. Dr. No explained that Matt could not be made to do anything that he did not want to do and the purpose of hypnosis in a criminal case was merely to clarify the images that were seen by the witness because the mind had recorded the incident. He asked Matt for permission to videotape the session because one of the challenges in a court would be whether or not the power of suggestion was used to get a witness to remember a specific fact relating to the crime.

The doctor told Matt that he would simply be in a light sleep and asked if he was ready to begin. When Matt said he was, the Doctor threw the switch to turn on the camera and the audio.

Matt was told to close his eyes and just relax. The doctor told him he was walking down a path in a rainforest and that Matt could feel the cool damp breeze on the back of his neck. He told Matt to look up into the trees and see the leaves on the trees dripping moisture. He told him to continue to walk down the path and he would see a pristine lake with water as far as the eye could see. He told Matt to place his right hand into the water of the lake and feel the cold refreshing water at which point Matt shivered slightly, letting the doctor know that he was under the hypnosis.

The doctor told Matt he was in Cincinnati, Ohio at the Smale Park and asked what Matt was seeing. Matt told him that he was looking at the waterfall on the rock wall with the pastel colors in the background. Matt said he was turning and now looking out onto the Ohio River which was totally dark except for the barge that was slowly passing by.

The doctor told Matt he wanted him to walk back to the hotel, up Walnut Street and to tell him if he saw or heard anything. Matt's expression changed as he told the doctor he heard the sound of a woman moaning in an alley off to his right at which point the doctor asked what Matt saw when he looked down the alley. Matt said he saw a something laying on the ground in the alley and the silhouette of a man running in the opposite direction away from where Matt was standing. The Doctor told Matt to focus his concentration on what was laying in the alley and that he would be able to see it clearly. Matt immediately reported that he saw a woman with long dark color hair, a pale blouse with a large stain, dark color skirt and black stiletto heels laying on the ground in the middle of the alley. Next the doctor told Matt to focus his total attention on the man running away and to tell him what he saw. Matt's eyes squinted as he looked down the alley and he told the doctor that it was a man of medium height and a slim build, wearing a long sleeve dark colored shirt and dark pants. Matt told the doctor that there was something odd about the way the man was running, like the man had a limp or one leg was shorter than the other. The doctor asked Matt what else he saw. Matt replied that there was some kind of object in the guy's left hand and that the guy turned left out of the alley. The doctor told Matt to focus totally on the running man's face and asked if Matt could see the man's face. Matt twitched in the chair and said the running man turned toward him for only a split second, but that he could see the man was white.

The doctor told Matt that Matt would awaken and feel relaxed and have a vivid recollection of what he had seen and began counting backwards from five. When he reached the number one, Matt opened his eyes.

The doctor told Matt that the video would be sent to Cincinnati PD by Corporal Berry and that he had done well. Matt thanked the doctor and quietly left the office.

Matt got into his car and felt relaxed and really good about what he just experienced. He decided to take a ride to the bar near the campus and see if Margot might be working. He still had not gotten her phone number.

***

Grenko wandered into the office to start his day feeling sluggish and out of sorts. He made a beeline for the coffee pot that was located in the back of the office passing by his desk with the phone message lamp flashing in such a manner as to attach a sense of urgency that he listen to the message. The call was from a detective in the Los Angeles County, California Sheriff's Department who said he was given Grenko's name and number by the Cincinnati Homicide Commander. The detective said that he had information on a homicide involving a witness who lived in LA and that Grenko needed to call him at his earliest convenience. The LA cop was laughing as he reminded Grenko that if he played this message first thing in the morning that it would be five am on the west coast. Grenko put the number in his pda and set the phone alarm for eleven o'clock to remember to call and then went to the back to fill his coffee cup.

It was just after eleven when Rudy Grenko made the call. Cpl. Berry told him that a man who said he was a witness to a Cincinnati Homicide had called the LASO and asked about hypnosis. Berry told the Cincy detective that he had set up the session and was sending the video of it overnight in a secure evidence envelope with a chain of custody via FedEx, but that he could also send it via e-mail for the detectives to watch. Cpl. Berry hoped that there would be information of value to the Cincinnati case and wished Grenko success in finding the badguy.

Almost all of the Homicide dicks were in the conference room to watch the video he had received. Grenko and Weeman had their note pads on the hope that something on the screen would give them some direction as their investigation was pretty much going nowhere to this point.

Most of the people in the room had never witnessed a hypnosis session and their participation was solely based on curiosity.

As they saw the witness recalling what he had seen in that alley on the night that JoAnn Wordly was murdered, Grenko and Weeman both lit up when they heard the direction of travel that the suspect took because it gave them new information they could pursue. The suspect had run north on Main Street and both the Federal Building and Post Office are located at Fifth and Main Streets and both have sophisticated surveillance systems which would likely have picked up some activity.

Grenko contacted the U.S. Postal Police while Weeman called the Federal Protective Service who protected the Federal Building and asked for their video of the corner of Fifth and Main between the hours of ten thirty and eleven fifteen pm on the night Wordly was killed. As soon as both agencies had the time isolated, the investigators went a picked up the cd's and took them back to the office.

The tape from the Post Office showed a man walking up Main Street from where the alley was at three minutes after eleven. The man had a bit of a limp on his right side which is something that the witness identified in the hypnosis session and the clothing was a match as well.

The high quality of the equipment used by the Feds gave a decent view of the face of the man, but Cincinnati has a Video Enhancement

Unit which might be able to zoom in and get a good face picture. The VEU was able to isolate a picture and the Public Information Office released the picture to all of the media outlets for broadcast as a person of interest in the homicide. Cincinnati was one of the first cities in the country to establish a Crimestoppers hotline based on the model developed in Texas. Crimestoppers offers a cash reward for information leading to an arrest and the caller is able to remain anonymous with volunteer citizens paying out the cash reward to a caller based on a number given to the caller.

The photo aired on local television station news broadcasts at four, five, five-thirty, six and eleven and the calls started coming in to Crimestoppers which was now in its thirtieth year in Cincinnati. One of the callers told the operator that the picture looked like a guy named William Clanton who lived on Twentieth Street in Covington, Kentucky, just across the bridge from Cincinnati.

When the two detectives got that information they immediately called Covington Police and asked if they had any information on Clanton. Covington records showed that a William Clanton, a thirty-seven year old white male who lived at 118 West 20th Street had been arrested twice. One arrest was for public drunkenness and the other was a domestic assault involving a former girlfriend. Clanton had been convicted of the public intoxication, but was acquitted in the assault case because the victim did not show up for court.

Grenko and Weeman drove across the Suspension Bridge into Covington, Kentucky. The Suspension Bridge is historic because the Brooklyn Bridge in New York was designed after it. As they were crossing the bridge, Weeman reminded his Sergeant that JoAnn's diary talked about her relationship with an older man and that things were starting to come together.

It was a bit ironic that Clanton's home address is only about two blocks from Covington Police Headquarters. The detectives went to the PD to ask for a uniform car since they were in another state and had no jurisdiction or authority. Covington PD provided two uniform officers to escort the detectives to Mr. Clanton's address to see if he was home.

The two cars pulled up in front of the address and the four officers went to the front door. One of the uniform cops knocked on the door and a man in his late thirties wearing a t-shirt and shorts answered the door. Grenko immediately took notice that the guy's right leg appeared to be a bit shorter than his left, something that the witness had identified during the hypnosis.

The man who answered the door identified himself as William Dwight Clanton. Clanton told the cops that his parents named him after former President Dwight Eisenhower. Grenko asked Clanton if he would accompany them to Covington PD headquarters to help them in an investigation that they were conducting into a murder which occurred recently in Cincinnati. Grenko knew that he could not take him to Cincinnati since that would require extradition and hoped that this suspect would go along voluntarily.

The Covington cops transported Clanton back to their station and took him into an interview room so the Cincinnati cops could interrogate him. The interview room was also equipped with audio and video recording capability.

Specialist Weeman opened a folder and removed a picture of JoAnn Wordly that had been found on Wordly's Facebook page and asked Clanton if he knew her. Clanton hesitated for a short time and told the investigators that he might have seen her somewhere, but could not remember where or when that might have been. Clanton's body language and facial expression indicated that he was suddenly very uncomfortable and the two Cincinnati cops decided it was time to read Clanton his Miranda warnings. Clanton refused to sign the written waiver but he had not asked to be speak with a lawyer and the cops would have the video evidence that the warnings had been given if that became an issue later.

Grenko told Clanton that there had been a witness to the murder in the alley and that the witness had described a man running away who fit Clanton's general description. The Sergeant then opened his folder and produced the surveillance photo of a man who looked just like Clanton. Willie Clanton denied vigorously that he had been in Cincinnati that night and told the two cops that he had been in a couple of Covington bars until they closed at three in the morning. Clanton told the cops that he could not remember the names of the bars he had been in or name anyone that had seen him that night.

Weeman then asked if Mr. Clanton had ever visited anyone on Mustang Drive. Rather than ask the detectives where Mustang Drive was located, Clanton nervously told the two cops that he didn't think so. The cops knew they had the right guy and now it was just a matter of getting him to admit to it. Weeman told Clanton that there was a nosey neighbor next door to the house on Mustang who probably would be able to identify the man she had seen entering and leaving the house if she was shown a photo lineup at which point Clanton told the investigators that he did know JoAnn Wordly and had been to her house a few times. Clanton said he did not want to admit that at first because the cops asking him questions about her murder scared him. Clanton said he would not do anything to harm that nice young girl.

The investigators asked Clanton if he would like something to drink since they were going to leave the room to get themselves a cup of coffee and Clanton's lips looked dry and parched. Clanton asked for a soda and the two cops left to get the drinks for all. They walked out of the interview room and went into an adjoining room which had a one way mirror looking into the interview room. They silently watched Clanton who was visibly shaken and nervous sitting in the chair.

Grenko contacted the Hamilton County Prosecutor's Office and was told that he had enough to obtain an arrest warrant and to ask Covington PD to hold Clanton while the warrant was obtained. A Covington detective offered to get the two Ohio cops a search warrant for the residence of Willie Clanton and drove them to the Commonwealth Attorney's office in Covington to draw up the warrant. The Commonwealth Attorney is the name for the County Prosecutor in Kentucky.

Clanton was taken by Covington PD to the Kenton County Jail for extradition into Ohio on a Murder charge.

***

The Covington detective and the two Cincinnati cops filled out the request for a warrant to search for clothing and the weapon used in the homicide in Cincinnati at the residence of William Dwight Clayton. A Kenton County, Kentucky Judge signed the warrant and the Covington detective placed a call to have their crime scene technicians waiting at the house on 20th Street.

There were several members of the Covington Police Department waiting at the address when the three detectives pulled up. That included the Covington PD crime scene van and techs wearing blue overalls with gloves and shoe covers so as not to contaminate the scene. Officers announced their intent to enter and when no one responded, they entered through the unlocked front door. The house was what is known as a row house, one built in the early 1900's where all of the houses are in close proximity to each other. The house was not well kept and the furniture was tattered and torn.

The crime scene techs conducted a methodical room by room search looking for bloody clothing or the weapon used to kill JoAnn Wordly. They swabbed the inside of the washer for traces of human blood. After an almost four hour intensive search nothing related to the homicide was found. As everyone was preparing to leave, a Covington uniformed cop asked if anyone had seen a trash can because trash day was tomorrow. A garbage can was located in the rear of the house and it was overfull. The techs turned over the can onto the back lawn and began looking thru the accumulated trash when they came upon a navy blue long sleeve shirt which appeared to be covered in blood. The techs placed the bloody shirt inside a brown paper bag, sealed the bag with tamper-proof evidence tape and handed the bag to a Covington detective.

The Cincinnati cops would have to be present at a hearing the next morning in a Kentucky courtroom to see if Clanton would be willing to waive extradition to Ohio or would decide to challenge the extradition request.

The two Ohio cops drove back to end their day and were ecstatic at the accomplishments of the day.

CHAPTER SEVEN

William Dwight Clanton appeared before a Kentucky Judge and waived an Extradition Hearing allowing the Cincinnati detectives to take him back with them to Ohio.

They took him to the C.I.S. office and put him in another interview room leaving him sit in the empty room for almost thirty minutes to let his nerves get the best of him.

The two detectives entered the small room with two cups of coffee and a can of Pepsi for Clanton, who was perspiring profusely even though the air conditioning in the room was working perfectly. Detective Weeman had a brown grocery bag in his right hand that was covered at the top with red tape with the word EVIDENCE printed on the tape. Weeman set the closed bag on the table.

Weeman had noticed that when Clanton had signed the extradition waiver in Kentucky that he did so with his left hand. Grenko placed the cold Pepsi can in the center of the table to see which hand Clanton would use to pick it up. Clanton picked up the can with his left hand and the investigators had verified another piece of the statement of the witness who had reported seeing an object in the suspect's left hand as he was running from the alley.

Grenko told Clanton that it was only going to be a matter of time until they could tie Clanton to a romantic relationship with the young woman and that the investigators believed that they knew the motive for killing her. Clanton simply stared at the floor and made no comment or showed any emotion to the investigators startling statements.

They repeated that Clanton had the right to have an attorney present at any time during the questioning and that Clanton would appear before an Ohio Judge the next morning for arraignment on the charge of Murder. The investigators took notice of the fact that Clanton had not once looked at the bag sitting on the desk or asked what it contained.

Weeman decided to give Clanton some clue as to where the investigation was headed in the hope of getting a reaction. Weeman told Clanton that the coroner had determined that JoAnn had sex with someone within twenty-four hours prior to her death and that a swab taken from her vagina would give DNA as to who her sex partner was. He then asked Clanton if he would voluntarily give a DNA sample so that Clanton could be excluded as the sex partner, to which Clanton declined. Weeman told Clanton that it really did not matter since the investigators were going to get a court order for him to give DNA anyway.

Rudy Grenko leaned back in his chair and took a sip from his coffee. In a tone almost like an afterthought, Grenko asked Willie if he had any interest in the contents of the brown bag sitting on the desk. When Willie nodded that he was interested, the Sergeant told Willie that the Covington cops had obtained a warrant to search Willie's house. Although the Covington cops were not able to find anything of interest inside the house, they did find something in the bottom of the garbage can in the rear of the house and asked Willie if he had any idea what that could be.

Willie broke down at that moment and his pea sized brain told him he should have followed his instinct and burned the damn shirt. His eyes told the two cops in the room that he was ready to talk to them.

Weeman told Willie that the shirt would be sent to a lab where the blood and DNA on the shirt would surely be that of JoAnn and that he might as well tell what really happened that night.

Tears streamed down Willie's face as he told the cops that he had gone to the house on Mustang in the early evening, entering through a rear door that the old lady never locked. He found her sitting in a chair watching television and snuck up on her and snapped her neck. He waited until it was completely dark, so the nosey broad next door would not see him, to take the body of the woman out to her car and throw her in the trunk. He then went back to his car and got a fifty pound bag of kitty litter which he emptied into the trunk of the car to mask the smell of the dead body because he had seen that done on a television show. Willie told the cops he threw the keys to the car in the trunk with the body.

He then went downtown to meet JoAnn after she got off work. He told her he would walk her to her car and asked him to marry him because he knew that the settlement money would now be totally her's and he would be set for life. He told the investigators that they were at the alleyway when she said there was no way she would ever marry him. He was just a playmate for her. Willie told the cops that he went into a rage and dragged JoAnn into the alley where he pulled a knife from his pocket and stabbed her twice before running out of the alley and back to his car.

The two investigators had gotten Willie to confess, so they called for a uniform car to take him from the C.I.S. office to the Hamilton County Justice to be housed until the arraignment the next morning.

***

It was a super-hot morning in the Los Angeles region and Matt was sitting in a lawn chair watching the beach bunnies and beach bums playing sand volleyball in an open area when his cell phone rang. Matt picked up the cell and the caller id had a ten digit number with the first three being 513. Matt did not know where the 513 area code originated and just assumed it was going to be a wrong number.

Rudy Grenko had arrived at the office with an energy level that he had not felt in years. He checked the file to retrieve the cell phone number of the kid who had been the witness to the murder that he had just solved. He picked up the office phone and then thought it would be really tacky to call at what would be five am on the west coast. He told his partner that they needed to be at court for the arraignment of Willie Clayton at nine am and then they could grab some breakfast after which Rudy would call the kid in California.

The arraignment lasted less than two minutes at which time the Judge set Willie's bond at two million dollars cash only. A team of investigators had gone to Mustang Drive the night before and had Danise Davis' vehicle towed to the coroner's lab to have a pristine crime scene. When the lab opened the trunk, they found exactly what Willie had told the investigators in the interview.

Matt said hello into the phone and the caller identified himself as Rudy Grenko from the Cincinnati Police Homicide Section, reminding Matt that they had eaten lunch together while Matt was in Cincinnati taking the police tests. Matt said that he remembered and asked how he could help the investigator. Rudy told Matt he only called to tell Matt that, based on information Matt had provided, an arrest had been made in the murder Matt witnessed and that prosecutors would be seeking the death penalty as the case led to the discovery of a second related murder and Rudy wanted to thank Matt for his cooperation. Rudy also told Matt that the commander of the Homicide Unit was in the process of writing a letter to the Police Chief detailing Matt's cooperation and hoped that it would help Matt get hired with the Cincinnati Police.

After Matt hung up the phone with the Cincinnati cop, he grabbed his stuff and ran toward his car because he wanted to tell his parents in person about the call he had just received. His mind was racing a mile a minute as he drove toward his house. He was not even thinking about how fast he was driving until he heard the short blasts of a siren and looked in the rear view mirror to see an LAPD motorcycle behind him with the red and blue lights flashing.

The LA traffic cop got off his motorcycle smiling because this would be the easiest ticket he would write all day. When he got to the driver's side door of the Mustang, the cop asked for Matt's driver's license, registration and proof of insurance. Matt handed the requested items to the motor cop and apologized for his speed telling the officer that he was hurrying home to tell his parents that a Cincinnati, Ohio cop had just called with some great news. The LA motor cop had a puzzled look on his face until Matt told him that he had been in Cincinnati testing to be a cop there and had witnessed a murder. The call from the cop in Cincinnati was to tell him that they had made an arrest in the case. The motor cop's face went from a smile to a scowl as he handed Matt back all his cards and told him to have a nice day.

Matt had been introduced to the world of professional courtesy.

Matt felt like he was floating on air as he ran up the steps to his house only to find that his father was still at his job. He would wait until dinner to tell them what had happened leaving out the part of being stopped for speeding, of course.

CHAPTER EIGHT

Matt looked at the clock and did what he had done every day for the past four weeks on days where there was mail delivery. He walked to the door and looked down the walkway waiting for the letter carrier to arrive with the family's daily mail.

The letter carrier entered the walkway and broke into a big smile on his face and a single envelope in his right hand. As he approached Matt, he asked Matt if this was the reason that he waited for him for these many days. The envelope had the logo of the City of Cincinnati clearly visible in the top left corner and the words Cincinnati Civil Service Commission next to it. Matt had to sign for the letter as it was sent certified mail.

Matt ripped the seal on the envelope almost tearing the letter itself. The letter was dated two days earlier and said.

> The Cincinnati Civil Service commission is pleased to make a conditional offer of employment as a Cincinnati Police Officer. This offer is contingent upon your successful completion of a background investigation and completion of the training program.

The Police Academy class will begin on September 14th and you will be required to be a resident of Ohio at the time of being sworn in as a police officer.

There will be an orientation program that will begin on September 7th during at which time you will be fitted for uniforms and provided the necessary equipment to perform the function for which you were hired.

Once again, congratulations on your appointment. You have ten days from the date of receipt to notify this commission of your acceptance which can be completed by e-mail or online at the Cincinnati government website.

Sincerely,

Civil Service Commission

Matt was sorry that no one was home and wanted to run out into the front yard and scream at the top of his lungs. The letter carrier had stayed at the entrance while Matt read the letter and Matt hugged the man who he didn't even know.

Once the euphoria had subsided, Matt was overwhelmed with both anticipation and fear. He had never lived on his own, never cooked his own meal, washed his clothes or even made his own bed. He would have to find a place to live, get furniture and dishes and silverware and he would be more than two thousand miles from his parents. He was beginning to get more scared by the minute.

Matt decided not to accept the offer at this moment, but to sit down with his parents and let them help him strategize his future. He felt his heartbeat double with fear and anticipation.

Matt laid the letter on the dining room table so that whoever got home first would see it as they entered.

When his father got home and saw the letter, he told Matt that the family should go out for dinner and celebrate this event. His mother threw her arms around Matt and broke into tears, telling him that the tears were of joy, not sadness. Dad called for reservations at Matt's favorite restaurant and the family dressed up for the occasion.

After enjoying the meal in the restaurant, the discussion focused on Matt's future plans. Matt's parents told him that they would loan him the money necessary to get started in Cincinnati. Matt would need to drive from Los Angeles to Cincinnati if he wanted to have his car. His mother offered to fly to Cincinnati and help him buy the things that he will need to get started in an apartment. Over the two months that they had until he started his new job, mom would teach him some of the things he would need to survive on his own. The decision of the family was that he should accept the offer from Cincinnati.

Matt made a commitment to learn everything he could about the new city he would be moving to and to start looking for an apartment immediately. Matt had never seen his parents look this happy and he felt empowered to be successful for them and all the sacrifices they made to get him to this point.

When they arrived home Matt went directly to his room and began looking at apartments available in Cincinnati. Not knowing anything about what neighborhoods were safe and what were not presented an issue that he would have to find a way to address.

***

The days passed quickly for Matt as he prepared to move his whole life to Cincinnati. His mother had him help her cook each night and he learned how to make some basic dishes that would sustain him so that he didn't have to eat in restaurants every night. She also taught him how to separate and wash and dry laundry and he helped wash dishes for the first time in his life.

Matt decided that he wanted to be in Cincinnati prior to the Labor Day weekend because he had found on the web that Cincinnati hosts an annual event called Riverfest on the Sunday before the holiday. Riverfest draws over three hundred thousand people to the Ohio River for a day of fun ending in a fireworks display. Cincinnatians call it the official end of summer and it sounded like something that Matt would like to see.

Matt found a studio apartment in the center of the downtown area with a security system and was under seven hundred dollars a month. Matt had some comfort level of the downtown area and had enjoyed his visit to the riverfront area which had been completely rebuilt over the past few years. He would be able to walk to Great American ballpark to watch the Cincinnati Reds baseball team or to Paul Brown Stadium to watch the Cincinnati Bengals football team and he would only be three miles from the Police Academy training facility. The apartment would be available after August 25th and Matt could lock it in by sending a check with the first month's rent and a one month security deposit.

Everything Matt owned would fit into the Mustang as he only had clothing, his laptop computer and his television set to take with him. Matt would allow three days for travel and wanted to make it a leisurely ride across the country. His mother would fly into

Cincinnati, or rather Kentucky, on August 28th to help him purchase the furniture and other items he would need.

Matt's cross country drive was an experience he would always remember and cherish. He got to drive through the beautiful parts of Arizona, New Mexico and Texas where he ended his first day. The second day took him into Oklahoma and through Missouri and into Illinois. The last leg of the trip covered Indiana and ended in Cincinnati. The total trip ran just over two thousand two hundred miles.

Matt had purchased an air mattress that he could sleep on in the new apartment until his mother arrived. Matt's view from his third floor apartment was a Catholic church that was constructed in the late 1800's made of granite and stone. The apartment was located on Sycamore Street between Sixth and Seventh which is at the eastern end of the downtown business district. He was less than two blocks from the heart of the City which is Fountain Square

Matt suggested to his mother that she make a reservation at a downtown hotel since he only had the air mattress in the apartment. Matt spent his first few days just driving around looking at the City. He drove across all three bridges that took him into Kentucky and drove the one hundred mile circle freeway that took him into southeastern Indiana and the northern and eastern corners that surrounds Cincinnati.

***

Matt was waiting at the end of the terminal for his mother to arrive. Matt knew that his parents had skipped taking vacations to save the money needed to pay for his education and wanted to make this a special trip for his mom.

As they drove north toward the city, Matt felt like a tour guide explaining to his mother the sites of Covington, Kentucky and the skyline of Cincinnati. Matt pointed out the sports facilities and the water traffic passing slowly on the Ohio River. He drove straight to his new apartment so that he could leave his car in the indoor garage and they could walk to the hotel where his mom would be staying.

Matt's mom looked at the spacious studio apartment and told Matt that it would not require a lot of furnishing. She envisioned a bed, dresser and a small table at one end, a couch and lounge chair in the middle with the flatscreen television mounted on the wall and a small dining room table just off the kitchen. The building had a laundry room in the basement, so that negated the need for that purchase. They would go out the next day to purchase the furnishings for the new place.

Matt grabbed his mom's luggage and they walked the two blocks to her hotel. She marveled at the Tyler Davidson Fountain that is the centerpiece of Fountain Square and the peacefulness of the Square itself. They got her checked in to the hotel and dropped her luggage in the room. Matt told his mom that she needed to actually taste Cincinnati style chili and that the secret ingredient in it was cinnamon. His mom chose to skip the onions and beans and just have the chili with spaghetti and cheese. She really liked it.

Matt escorted his mom back to the hotel and told her to take a nap because of the long cross country flight and that they would check out the river in the evening hours where she could see the new park and the skylines of Kentucky and Ohio. Mom looked tired and ready for a nap. Matt walked back to his apartment feeling really good about his new life and home.

Matt walked into the lobby of the hotel just after seven p.m. and picked up the house phone to call his mother's room. He thought that he would take her to a Japanese steak house on Sixth Street and then they could walk down to the park. Since the Cincinnati Reds were also playing a game at home, she would be able to see Great American Ballpark lit up and the area would be bustling with people.

As they were walking down Walnut Street toward the new Smale Park, Matt stopped at the alley between Fourth and Fifth to show his mom where the murder that he had witnessed occurred. They continued on to the Park and Matt's mom could see the people streaming into the ballpark for the Reds baseball game and the activity around the restaurants and bars that were just across the street from the stadium. The two wandered the park and walked all the way down to the river which was dark, but peaceful. She was amazed at the view of the skyline of Northern Kentucky and the boats that were moored on the opposite side of the river. After three hours of wandering aimlessly around the riverfront, mom told Matt she was tired and wanted to get back to her hotel. She kissed him on the cheek and was wearing a big smile as she got on the elevator to go up to her room.

Matt returned to his apartment and opened his computer. He had a list of things that needed to be done before his orientation that was just one week away. He had already notified the Civil Service Commission of his Cincinnati address, but had yet to obtain an Ohio driver's license and transfer his vehicle registration to Ohio, but decided that those things could wait until after his mother left to return home. He was still awaiting installation of his telephone service.

Since arriving in Cincinnati Matt had decided not to check out the nightlife and remain low key so that he could avoid getting into any trouble before he started his new career. He mostly just stayed in the apartment and watched television or drove aimlessly around the city to familiarize himself with the new culture, which was completely different than that he had known from the west coast.

***

He was in the lobby of the hotel early the next morning to go furniture hunting with his mother. He drove her to the Frisch's Restaurant where the Homicide guys had brought him for lunch and they relaxed and enjoyed the breakfast bar.

They were able to find a couch that would accept his six foot frame and a lounge chair that reminded him of the one in the hypnotist's office, Mom picked out a small cherry wood dining table that was sort of small but claimed to seat four and the last item they purchased was a queen size bed with electronics to change the temperature and vibrate to relax muscles. The items would be delivered the next day and mom would be there to help him effectively place them before she was flying back to Los Angeles. Matt was going to be sorry to see her leave. He had never in his life felt this close to his family as he did at this moment.

Matt drove his mom around Cincinnati showing her Music Hall, which for decades was the cultural center of Cincinnati. He drove her to Union Terminal, which had once been one of the largest railroad centers in the United States and now housed a Museum. His mom marveled at the architectural beauty and history of Cincinnati, Ohio.

When they went into the Clifton area of the city, Matt showed her the campus of the University of Cincinnati, sprawling greenery in the heart of an urban city. They drove through Burnet Woods, a park with a mirror lake located just across from the north side of the campus and looked at some of the treasured vintage houses that were near the campus as well. His mom wanted to see the location of the central police station and quizzed him on who Ezzard Charles was. She was actually mildly surprised when Matt knew the answer.

As they were enjoying a leisurely dinner, Matt's mom told him that a Cincinnati Police investigator had come to their house the day before she left to come to Cincinnati. The investigator told her and his dad that he was in LA for two days doing a background check for Matt's employment as a Cincinnati cop. The investigator said he had already been to Matt's high school and UCLA and had spoken with the surrounding neighbors. The investigator said his inquiry had turned up nothing that would knock Matt out of the process. Matt didn't realize that a city would actually pay to send an investigator across the country to learn about him and this solidified his belief that the job was his if he completed the training, which should be a breeze for him.

Matt received a call the next morning telling him that the furniture would arrive between one and three p.m. that day. He called his mom at her hotel and told her he would meet her for lunch and they could walk back to his place to meet the movers. He told her he knew this perfect little hole in the wall called the Orange Bar and she would love it. They walked into the place, got their hot dogs and ate on Fountain Square. Since his mom had a six fifteen flight home, the day had fallen perfectly into place and Matt would have a real bed to sleep in tonight.

As she kissed him goodbye at the airport, Matt's mom promised that both his parents would be in Cincinnati for his graduation ceremony from the Police Academy.

CHAPTER NINE

Matt arrived at the Police Academy training facility fifteen minutes early for his orientation week. He had decided to wear the same outfit that his mother had chosen for his interviews.

He counted forty-five people attending the orientation to participate in the training program consisting of six women and thirty-nine men. They appeared to range in age from people who were his age to the oldest who appeared to be in his mid to late thirties. The group was varied in physical stature from those who looked like they worked out regularly to a couple that Matt had to wonder how they had passed the grueling run and agility portion of the testing. It was going to be an interesting and diverse class.

The program opened with a six minute video from the Mayor of Cincinnati, the honorable Mark Mallory, who welcomed the new employees to the city and told of the vision and dreams of the city leading into the future.

The first speaker was a woman from the Human Resources Office of the City of Cincinnati. She opened with the benefits package that the new employees would receive which included health, dental and vision. She told them that the City had a mandatory direct deposit policy and that each new employee would have to have a bank account that their payroll could be deposited into. Since Matt had just arrived in Cincinnati, and the fact that he had never had a checking account before, Matt felt some concern over this until the lady told everyone that the Cincinnati Police had its own credit union which fulfilled the requirement. She next discussed the fact that public employees in Ohio did not pay into the Federal Social Security program, but paid into the State of Ohio Police and Fireman's Disability Pension Fund. They would receive a full retirement once they had accrued twenty-five years of service and reached forty-eight years of age. They would be vested in the pension once they had completed five years of service. She received a round of applause when she told the group that this would be the easiest week they would have in their employment with the city and that the city would be providing lunch for everyone the first day.

The next speaker walked up to the podium wearing a police uniform with sergeant stripes on her sleeves. Sgt. Kate Harrison identified herself as the President of Queen City Lodge 60 of the Fraternal Order of Police and told the recruits that her full-time job was representing Cincinnati cops. She explained that membership in the F.O.P. was mandatory and that monthly dues would be automatically deducted from the officers paycheck because the F.O.P. was the official bargaining agent for all Cincinnati cops below the rank of Captain. She told the group that her salary and benefits were paid by the City through the donation of sick days by all of the officers in the

Police Department and she invited all of the class to visit the F.O.P. headquarters on Central Parkway to meet the elected officers of the F.O.P. and interact with other Cincinnati cops.

Next to speak was the Chief of Police who welcomed the recruits into the field of law enforcement and the service that they would be offering to the people of Cincinnati in protecting them and keeping them safe. James Craig talked about the start of his career with the Detroit, Michigan Police and how, when he was laid off, he transferred to Los Angeles Police where he spent twenty-six years and retired at the rank of Captain. Chief Craig then secured a Chief's position in Portland, Maine and then the Cincinnati position became available. Chief Craig told the recruits that effort and commitment to the profession presents many different career advancement opportunities, but only to those who are willing to work hard to be the best possible person and law enforcement professional. The Chief told the recruits that this was the first class since he became Chief and that it came about because he had streamlined the command staff, as well as eliminated redundancy in the Police Department, in order to devote more resources to street level policing. He ended by saying that the recruits journey would begin next Monday and he wished them a safe passage into the world of law enforcement.

After the box lunch that consisted of a ham or turkey sandwich, a small bag of chips and a piece of fruit, the group reconvened in the conference hall for the afternoon session. Matt got the opportunity to meet with just a few of his classmates. He had only exchanged small talk with them as they sat at a round table and ate.

When Matt got home from his first day of employment he felt he needed to celebrate his success so he went down to check out the restaurants and nightlife at the Banks Project that was designed to rejuvenate the downtown area and consisted of a collection of hotspots that had been recently opened across from the ballpark. He sat down at a table and ordered a beer. The waitress smiled pleasantly and asked him for identification to prove that he was over twenty-one, the legal drinking age in Ohio. Without giving it a thought, Matt produced his brand new identification card stating he is a Cincinnati Police Officer. The waitress blushed and left to get his beer. She returned in what seemed like seconds, set the beer and a frozen mug in front of Matt and told him that there was no charge per the direction of her manager. Matt was intensely concerned and embarrassed that he was being given a free drink because he was a cop, but did not know what he could do at this point. Matt decided to leave the price of the beer as a tip to the waitress and not to use that identification again for verification of his age.

Matt's group was the first to be fitted for their new uniforms. They would be fitted with their hat, shirts, gun belt, pants and shoes to prepare for their first classroom day. The group then toured the police property room, mounted patrol, the central police station and the substation that was in the Banks Project area.

Matt picked up the fitted uniforms on Friday afternoon and took them and neatly hung them in his closet for wear.

***

Matt pulled into the police academy parking lot with twenty minutes to spare. He had been scared to pick up coffee on the off chance that he would spill it onto his brand new uniform.

The receptionist directed him to his new classroom and he saw the sign above the door which stated:

THROUGH THESE DOOR PASS THE FINEST POLICE OFFICERS IN THE COUNTRY

He entered the classroom to see that there were students already in their seats. Each desk had a nameplate on the front facing forward and Matt found that they were in alphabetical order. Being as quiet and inconspicuous as possible, Matt sat down at his new desk and took stock of the items sitting in front of him. On the desk was one five inch thick binder which was empty, note paper and a pen with the logo of the Cincinnati Police Department. Matt had brought, as had others, a laptop computer to record his notes, but there was no place on the desk to fit it, so he placed it in a basket under his seat.

The room was now filling with the students of the new class and Matt sat quietly and sized up the incoming students as well as the ones already in their chairs. Matt took notice that several appeared, by their demeanor and dress, to be former military people. Everyone was focused on their posture as they awaited the start of the program. It was clear to Matt that everyone in the room was both nervous and excited.

At exactly eight o'clock a man in his forties wearing a Cincinnati Police uniform entered the room and closed the classroom door behind him. He introduced himself as Lieutenant Steven Salver and that his job was commander of the Police Training Unit of the Cincinnati Police Department. He welcomed all of the students into the family known as the Cincinnati Police Department and that he would be explaining to them how their training would proceed.

In a stern and authoritative voice the Salver ordered them out of their seats and to stand at attention. Salver told the class that every time the classroom door opened they were to immediately get up and stand at attention until told to sit back down. They were told that it did not matter whether the person entering the room was the Police Chief, an instructor or a janitor coming in to empty the trash, they would give the person entering the classroom due respect and deference.

Salver told the recruits that this would be unlike any training that they ever received. It would be a challenge to all and much more difficult than obtaining a college degree. Salver explained that the classroom door was locked on the outside and that it closed every hour on the minute. If a recruit was not in the classroom when the door closed, they would have to sit in the hallway until the door reopened, and that behavior would not be tolerated if it happened more than once. Salver told the students to look around the room at the others seated in the desks because, as the program progressed, they would begin to see vacant chairs with the nameplates removed. Some would leave because a career in law enforcement was not what they expected, others would be leaving because they chose not to put in the time and effort needed to succeed. He told the group that the instructors had no duty to make the recruits successful, rather their obligation was to give each student every opportunity to succeed.

Recruits would be assigned a locker later in the morning and were expected to be ready for whatever the daily schedule called for. Each day would start at 0700 and would consist of stretching, exercise and a daily run that would get longer each week. The recruits would then have to shower and dress for the day's activities and remember that the classroom door would lock exactly at eight o'clock. The Police department did not provide running shoes and if a recruit did not own a pair, that tonight would be a good time to buy a pair of high quality shoes to avoid an unnecessary injury.

Their day would run until five o'clock each day. They would have one hour for lunch. They could bring their lunch, purchase items from the vending machines located in the break room, or leave the facility and go to one of the many restaurants nearby. There was also free coffee available for them, if they wanted, during the breaks that would be ten minutes for each hour of classroom. Recruits were told that, if they chose to eat lunch outside, that they were representing the Cincinnati Police and were accountable for their behavior, under the rules of conduct, that all Cincinnati Police Officers were required to adhere to.

The Lieutenant then explained the items that were on the desk in front of each student. The five inch thick binder was to be filled with the handouts from each module of training and separated from other modules. The notebook paper was for the students to take notes from the classroom instruction. Recruits would not be permitted to use a computer to take notes and the written notes were to be typewritten in a cohesive manner and then placed with the handouts for the subject taught. Under the notebook paper were several sheets listing the daily activities that the recruit would be performing.

The recruits would be attending the police academy for ten weeks. At the conclusion of those ten weeks, they would be assigned to work in a Police District for two weeks with a specially trained officer called a Field Training Officer (FTO). They would be riding without a gun belt or a badge, but were there to observe how the things that they had learned up to that point were put into action. Their FTO would file a report to the Training Unit on the recruit's performance and their ability to follow direction.

Their final fourteen weeks would take them up to the final examination and they would be required to pass two written tests. The first would be the Police Department internal examination and then they would have to pass an examination with the State of Ohio. They would also have to pass each of the skills sections of the training in order to be eligible to take the State written exam. Those would include: firearms, defensive driving, physical agility, defensive tactics and first aid. The determining factor in whether they would pass or fail was their competency and proficiency in the specific area.

The State would use a computer to determine two hundred and forty multiple choice questions from a bank of twelve hundred possible questions. The class would receive all twelve hundred questions and all possible answers in their time in the classroom. The State defines these as Student Performance Objectives. These SPO's would be identified by the individual instructor and the class should make sure that they had them separated from their other notes so that they would be able to study them for the State examination. Salver suggested to them that they might want to form study groups to prepare for the written examinations to come.

The Lieutenant then asked if the recruits had any questions and, as if on cue, the classroom door opened. The recruits jumped out of their seats and stood at attention as their first instructor entered the room. They were left standing while Lt. Salver and the instructor exchanged pleasantries and then the Lt. exited the room. The instructor told the recruits that they could now return to their seats. Clearly, a message had been sent to the recruits of who was really in charge.

Police Specialist Tom Hais had fourteen years on the job and, as students would later find out, had been involved in two police shootings less than a month apart. He told the class that he would be taking them through the history of law enforcement and some of the history of the Cincinnati Police Department. He opened by telling the class that the Cincinnati Police were one of the only urban police agencies in the country to have taken the two-way radios out of all of the police cars and relied on portable radios with shoulder microphones as the method of communicating between dispatchers and other officers since the early 1970's.

With Federal funding under the Law Enforcement Assistance Program, Cincinnati had designed a program called Community Sector Team Policing or COMSEC. The intent of the program was to make officers more visible to the public by not having to rely on communications from the vehicle. Relay towers were strategically placed throughout the city and two-way radios in the cars were replaced by portables that the officers would wear on their duty belts. That led to the policy of assigning the radio to the individual officer that was taken home each day after duty and offered the officer the ability to call the dispatch center at any time day or night.

Specialist Hais explained that if a person does not know the history of something, they could not know how it got to where it is today and that if one does not understand where it is today, they cannot know the direction it is taking. Hais had the room in shock when he told them that they already had a hero among them. Without identifying who it was, Hais told the class that one of them was instrumental in helping investigators solve a downtown murder while taking the testing for the job. All of the members of the class were looking around at each other trying to figure out who Hais was talking about and Matt was putting on his best face not to give any telltale sign that it was him.

When they were told to break for lunch one recruit announced that anyone who wanted to join him should go to the Wendy's on Gest

Street, not far from Spinney Field. David Markum had played high school and college football as a cornerback and had actually been invited to a Cincinnati Bengal tryout before taking the testing for the Police Department. The department already had two cops who had played professional football for the Bengals team. Danielle McQueen chimed in that she was going. She had served two tours in Iraq with the Army and left the service as a Sergeant. It would be a good opportunity for Matt to get acquainted with some of his classmates, so he decided to go and meet them there. Six of the new recruits sat together at a table. They felt they were being watched by the others in the restaurant because they were wearing the recruit uniform of the Cincinnati Police and it was an uncomfortable experience for the newbies.

Matt had writer's cramp from the copious notes that he had to take. Matt had listened to the Commander and made a separate sheet to write down each SPO that was identified. After the conclusion of his first day, he decided to drive to the FOP Lodge on Central Parkway to see the building since his uniform would be recognized by the cops that would be there. Sgt. Harrison was there and introduced him to a couple of retired cops who were seated at the bar having a cold beer. Matt just had soda because he was still in uniform and left after just a couple of minutes. Matt drove back to his apartment and made himself a hamburger and onion rings and turned on the television to help wind down. The news was on and he saw some of the investigators he had interacted with at the scene of what the anchor called "a robbery gone bad." Matt set up his laptop and began translating his scribbling into cohesive notes that any reader would be able to comprehend.

Matt did not learn much that he did not already know because one of the college classes he had taken was on the history of American Policing, but he really liked the historical perspective of the police department he was now employed by.

Matt decided he needed to go to a store and buy a coffee pot so he could have morning coffee before putting on his uniform. He did not want anyone to see him with an ugly spill on his clothes and get laughed at.

Matt reported to the academy at five minutes before seven wearing the gym shorts and gray tee shirt that he had been provided. The instructor told the class that the run portion would start at one mile and increase each week until they reached three miles. He told them that they would still have to be in the classroom on time, so the pace of their run would be key if they wanted to have time to shower and still make it.

Matt made it through his first week of training unscathed. Some instructors yelled at the class more than others, but Matt had not been the brunt of anyone's anger, at least not yet.

Over the first weekend Matt reflected on his first week of the police academy training and thought how much different it was than his college experience. In college he had attended a class for fifty minutes three times a week and had a reprieve to digest what he had been taught. In this setting, one police related subject was immediately followed by another and he was being slammed with information at a pace that was difficult for him to comprehend. He had received a compliment on the notebook he had kept, but was shocked when he was told that this was only the first of five five-inch thick binders that he would fill before he was done.

CHAPTER TEN

After he had taken his shower following the morning run, Matt walked into the classroom and found the atmosphere completely different. Recruits were actually chatting with each other and the room seemed more relaxed than it had been last week.

Matt walked over to where two males and a female were chatting and softly introduced himself to them. One of the males introduced himself as Bill Donnelan and he told Matt that he had been a cop in a suburban department for the past five years and came to Cincinnati for the pay increase. Matt asked Donnelan why he had to sit through the training if he was already state certified and was told that everyone, no matter how much experience they had, was required to attend Cincinnati's training program.

Matt saw the female looking him up and down. She introduced herself as Dawn Taylor and said she had joined Cincinnati after three years with the University of Cincinnati Police Department. The third male told Matt he was from Northern Ohio and moved to Cincinnati to be a policeman. Matt told the three that he had just moved to Cincinnati from LA and that he had a studio apartment downtown if they would be interested in forming a study group as the Lieutenant had suggested. All three said they would think about it and went to their seats as class was about to begin.

There was an empty seat in the classroom after the door had been closed and Matt figured the guy must be sick or was late and going to be in trouble this early on. The seat remained empty all day as the recruits spent another day feverishly taking notes.

As Matt was sitting down to eat his tv dinner, the lead story on the news was that Cincinnati Police had announced the arrest of a police recruit on a charge of domestic violence for beating and kicking his fiancé after allegedly finding her with another man in the apartment that they shared in Northside which is located in District Five. The Police Chief had announced that the recruit had been terminated from his job. The first casualty of the class had already occurred.

The recruits were told that they would be electing their internal command structure the following week that would consist of a class lieutenant, two sergeants and three squad leaders. The command structure would be responsible for leading the class all the way to graduation.

The recruits were also provided their second empty binder and Matt was surprised that his first one was already almost full. They would have classroom training for the next two weeks and move on to the Firearms portion of the program starting next Monday.

Matt was deeply disappointed when he was not elected to one of the class leadership positions but, after reflection, realized that the recruits who came from a law enforcement or military background had received training similar to that which he was experiencing for the first time. He would showcase his talents to his fellow students as the class progressed.

***

The firearm training facility is located in Evendale, Ohio, a small city at the north end of Cincinnati. The facility sits just off I-75 on seventy acres and includes the canine training area, building searches and an outdoor shooting range.

The morning run was conducted around the streets of Evendale, a combination residential community that is the home of a General Electric aviation plant that, at one time, employed more than eleven thousand workers.

A wry smile came to Matt's face when the two instructors walked into the classroom because they were the two brothers who had helped him through the physical agility portion of the testing process.

The first thing the recruits were told is that actual police shootings are nothing like what is seen on television. Few cops will ever fire their gun anywhere but at the range and police shootings are over in a little more than three seconds. There is no time to think about what will happen, so the cop will totally react to how they have been trained.

This would be the first time that Matt had actually worn his gun belt and he had never handled, much less fired, a weapon before. Matt actually envied the people who had come from a police or military background because they would be much more comfortable and have less fear. Sitting on the desks in the classroom were the recruits nameplates, a Smith and Wesson 9mm silver plated handgun and two empty magazines. Recruits had been told before they entered the classroom that they were not permitted to touch anything until told to by an instructor. Tim Hatterfeld welcomed the recruits to the facility and told them the next sixty hours would be devoted to teaching them about the use and deployment of deadly force. He explained that he would rather work with people who had never handled a firearm before because they had not yet developed bad habits causing Matt to feel a bit more comfortable about what was to come.

The recruits spent the first day of firearm training learning how to safely handle, load and unload the 9mm handgun. When they left for the day, the handguns were left on the desks for the instructors to put away safely. On the second day the class learned how to clear malfunctions that occur when using a semi-automatic handgun. Malfunctions occur because the gun will tend to jam when one bullet cartridge is not properly ejected or does not properly feed the next bullet into the chamber. The malfunction renders the weapon useless until it is cleared and the stress level is beyond description. Also, unlike television, one of the participants is not likely to survive the encounter. Put simply, there are no "second takes."

The third day was the first that the recruits would be firing live ammunition and the thought had Matt really nervous until his first shots fired actually hit the target where he was aiming. Matt felt really good about how well he was progressing until the instructor told the students that there would be time constraints set for them to draw their weapon from the holster and fire. Matt felt pure fear when he heard that the students would have an actual time of three seconds to draw and fire shots into the target. The firearm training would then move to multiple targets and all of the exercises would be timed. One of the students suffered a hand injury when he hit a metal stanchion with a bullet doing a shooting exercise from an arm's length away from the target. After being treated, the student was back in the training wearing just a small bandage on his non-shooting hand.

As the second week of the firearm training began, there was another empty seat. The recruits were just told that a female recruit had left voluntarily as she decided that this was not the career for her. Recruits were now moving and shooting at the same time and being placed in stressful situations so that, when something would occur in real life, they would react to how they had been trained.

The recruits were all administered the state required proficiency test and everyone passed. Matt took notice that, as each recruit went through the state proficiency test, that the class vocally supported the one being tested and that there was a sense of camaraderie developing that had not been there before. The next phase would be to learn how to search a building.

The recruits were teamed in pairs and had to enter a building to search for a burglar. Matt was paired with Dawn, the female recruit who he had chatted with before. They were told by the instructor that a witness had reported seeing a male enter the building, but had not seen him leave. The two recruits entered the dilapidated building with their guns drawn and, as they had been taught, identified themselves as police officers and ordered whoever was in the building to show themselves and their hands. When they received no answer, they would have to conduct a room by room search to find out if anyone was still in the building. The two recruits looked down a long dark hallway with doors on both sides leading to unknown rooms. They would have to methodically check each entrance without endangering their safety any more than absolutely necessary. Dawn said she would lead because she had actually done searches in her time with the University Police and it was Matt's job to protect her as she made entry into each room. She said once a room was cleared the door to that room would be closed so anyone wanting to enter would alert them by the sound of a door opening. She told Matt that there was no rush in the time they took. Their safety was paramount to everything else. Dawn opened the third door and saw a male dart into a back corner of the room where he could not be seen. She backed out of the room and gave Matt a signal that someone was in the room. She shouted commands for the person to come into her view and threatened to send a dog into the room to bite him if he did not come out immediately. The suspect came out, was handcuffed and taken out of the building. Two of the instructors were laughing uncontrollably since they knew there was no canine actually present. The instructors complimented Dawn on her creative action and the fact that they made the arrest without incident. Matt was thankful that he had gotten Dawn for a partner and offered to buy her a beer after the day's class.

As their firearm training came to a close, Matt saw a higher sense of confidence in the members of the class. They would return to the classroom empowered that they could succeed.

CHAPTER ELEVEN

The next several weeks passed quickly as the students learned the things that would be taking to the street in weeks eleven and twelve. Matt had been studying by himself and creating his own possible test questions that he would be able to use as a guide when it came time to take the final examination.

On the Friday at the end of week ten, the recruits were given their District assignments. The recruits would be paired with two different FTO's, one each week. The first week would be day shift and the second week would be on midnights. Their schedule would be four ten hour days and then off three days. They would wear their recruit uniforms and only carry a police portable radio. Matt would report to District Five at 0700 on Monday. District Five covered the University of Cincinnati campus northwest to the City line and he would be paired with a police officer named Don Luck. Luck was a fifteen year veteran who had been involved in the training of more than one hundred new recruits. He was an imposing figure and his voice commanded attention.

Matt arrived at the police station for his first shift, not really knowing what to expect. The briefing Sergeant welcomed the recruits assigned to District Five and issued the assignments for the shift, telling Luck and Matt that they would be working car 5104 and then went on to discuss the things, which had occurred over the past twenty-four hours. Their beat would actually be the University campus area.

When they got into the police car, Luck placed the key in the ignition and then stopped. He looked at Matt and told him not to take what Luck was about to say personally, but Matt needed to know that he was not in the police car to work as an officer. He was there only to observe and to learn. Luck explained that the radio designation had a specific meaning in Cincinnati. The first number identified the District, the second number identified the shift being worked and the last two numbers identified the area to be covered. They no sooner pulled out of the parking lot when they received a call to take a report of a burglary report at 221 Wheeler Street, just south of the campus. Luck explained that it was just a report where they would get the information on the burglary which had already occurred and there was no emergency.

Car 5104 pulled up to the front of the address, which was an older house in a neighborhood that provided off-campus housing to students of the university. Luck knocked on the front door and a young man in his late teens answered. The young man told the officers that this was a fraternity house and that he had returned to find the rear door had been pried open and that a computer and some cash had been taken from his room. He was the only one there, so he could not tell the officers if anything had been taken from anyone else. Luck asked the young man to show him the rear door and the officers were led to the open back entrance which and showed signs of being pried.

It had rained hard in Cincinnati early that morning and Matt took notice that there were footprints leading away from the rear door of the house. When he pointed out the footprints to Officer Luck, he and Luck followed the footprints through a yard and stopping at the rear door of a residence less than a block away from the house that was burglarized. Luck knocked on the rear door of the residence and then both officers heard the loud click that Luck immediately recognized as the sound of a shotgun being loaded to fire. Luck shoved Matt out of the doorway just as the pellets from the shotgun blast penetrated the wooden door. Luck drew his gun and radioed that he needed assistance, a term that tells the dispatcher that an officer is in trouble. Matt almost immediately heard the sound of multiple sirens getting louder with each second as police cars from anywhere close were screaming to get to them. There was a second blast from the shotgun and then silence from inside the house.

Luck pulled Matt away from the rear door and they took a position behind a rock wall at the house next door. There was screaming of tires coming to a stop and police officers were running toward the back of the house to aid the two officers. A supervisor arrived and immediately called out the SWAT team for a barricaded person. He directed officers into positions where the house was surrounded while they awaited the specially trained cops armed with automatic rifles and wearing helmets and military gear. A motor home arrived carrying a negotiator who would try to talk the person in the house to come out and end this peacefully. From his position behind the rock wall Matt could see news vans pulling up to the scene and police cars closing the surrounding streets to traffic. They remained in position for almost one and one-half hours at which point the commander of the SWAT team ordered his people to forcibly make entry into the house. When the team made entry into the house, they found a male dead in the kitchen who had apparently died from a self-inflicted gunshot wound to the face. The burglar had blown his own face off with the shotgun.

The scene was suddenly filled with cops. Matt saw one Assistant Police Chief, one Captain, two Lieutenants, and three Sergeants as well as homicide detectives. Matt and Luck would have to drive down to C.I.S. to file their statements of what had transpired. As they were driving downtown Luck looked at Matt and told him this was a great way to start his first day and then started laughing. They spent the shift answering the detectives questions and filing reports back at the District. Matt drove home with an adrenaline rush that he had never ever felt before.

Matt reported to District Five for his second shift after a night where he had slept very little. Matt had called Dawn to tell her about the incident and was shocked that she already knew about it. Dawn told Matt that the word was all over the police department and she was proud of the way he handled himself.

The two cops left the briefing room after getting their assignment for the day and cops were patting Matt on the back as they walked out to their patrol car. They would be working beat 5110, which covered the northwest limits of the city. They made a traffic stop and Luck showed Matt how to issue a traffic citation and the proper way to approach a vehicle on a traffic stop. The next call was to a traffic crash and Luck had Matt direct traffic around the scene while he took the report. Luck welcomed Matt into the mundane world of law enforcement.

Matt really appreciated that Luck made everything they did a teaching moment and prepared for his upcoming three days off. He would call home and catch up on his notes. Matt had already sent his parents two checks to repay them for the startup money they had provided and set up a savings program with the extra money he now had. He would be back at District Five on the night shift next week.

For the night shift Matt would be paired up a cop named Bill Silverman. Silverman told Matt that he knew about Matt's first day escapades and promised to try to make his week an easy one. He reiterated that Matt was still not a police officer and to simply do everything Silverman told him to and watch and learn.

As they rode around their beat and the traffic became less and less, Silverman told Matt to always be pro active and check areas where crime was likely to occur. Silverman said that, no matter what the weather was, Matt should keep the window down so he could he the sounds of his beat and to check behind businesses and look for things that are out of place. No sooner had he said that, the two found a rear window of an elementary school open. Silverman said that there is no way that two people could search a building of that size so he called and asked for a canine unit to make the search. The search did not uncover any evidence of a burglary and the officers closed the window and returned to patrol. In the subsequent days, Matt got the opportunity to participate in a D.U.I. arrest, arrested a man for domestic violence on his wife, and was involved in number traffic stops. He would return to his training with a much deeper understanding of the demands of the job.

CHAPTER TWELVE

Matt reported to the academy for his morning run and the receptionist told him the commander said for him to skip today's run and report to his office immediately.

The Lieutenant was seated at his desk and told Matt to sit down. Matt was scared that he was about to be kicked out of the class, but for what he had no clue. The Lieutenant looked up from the papers he was reading and told Matt that he had reviewed the complete incident report and that Matt would be asked by both the staff and the students to tell them what happened with the burglar who apparently took his own life. Matt was to tell anyone who asked that he was under orders of the police academy commander to talk to no one about the incident, including the Police Chief, and that any questions regarding what happened would be answered by the Lieutenant. Matt was told he could leave for breakfast or just get coffee and to be in the classroom before eight o'clock and that he was dismissed. Matt walked out of the commander's office relieved that he had not been thrown out but was confused as to the reason for the gag order.

When Matt walked into the classroom he was bombarded by questions from the recruits as to what happened, but could only say that he was not allowed to talk about it to anyone on orders of the

Lieutenant. As the class was breaking for lunch two instructors asked about the incident and he had to tell them the same thing,

Another chair was empty and no one seemed to know anything other than the male who had been there would not be returning.

Matt looked at the class schedule and saw that the mid-term written examination would be the following week so he approached several other recruits and asked about having a study group at his downtown apartment. Dawn and two others were interested and they would meet after class tonight. One would pick up pizza and another would bring beer and they would share the costs. Everyone would meet at six o'clock and they could work until ten or so. Matt had his separate binder that he kept with the possible test questions and he passed it around so that each person could ask a question from it to the person behind them. As it approached midnight the pizza and the beer were gone and they had to be ready for the run at seven, so they broke for the night with the promise to meet Saturday night to do it again. Matt felt like he was beginning to make some friends. Matt was looking forward to the next two days as they would be doing the defensive tactics portion from which the recruits would be trained in use of the PR-24 side handle baton, Taser and beanbag shotgun, all of which are less-than-lethal options. Matt knew of the Monadnock PR-24 from his college experience in discussions of the beating of Rodney King by Los Angeles cops and the "don't Tase me bro" video which went viral.

The group met again on Saturday night and didn't quit until two am after two trips for more beer. Matt offered the couch to one of the males who was a bit tipsy so he didn't get caught driving drunk and thrown out of the class, but Dawn offered to drive the recruit to his home because she had not drank at all. They agreed they were ready for the mid-term test.

The mid-term test scores were hanging on the wall of the classroom when Matt walked in. He had finished third overall, but there were two names with no scores at all. Matt looked toward the desks and saw two more nameplates missing. He was later told that both had failed the test. The class was now down to forty.

***

As the holiday season came closer and closer, Matt was really missing his mother's home cooking and seeing his parents. Since Christmas would fall on a Thursday this year and there would be no class scheduled for Christmas Eve or the day after the holiday, Matt made reservations to fly back to LA and surprise his parents with a seven day Pacific cruise he bought for them. He really wanted to deliver it personally to see the look on their faces.

Matt boarded the plane and thought of the warmth of the west coast since it was twenty-two degrees in Cincinnati. He would not arrive in LA until eleven p.m. coast time, so he told his parents he would rent a car and they would not have to pick him up from LAX.

Matt was reading a magazine when he heard a commotion coming from the front cabin and saw the stewardess struggling with a large Asian male. Matt jumped out of his seat and ran to the front where the male was screaming that he needed to get off the plane and was trying to open the hatch door. The plane was mid-air at approximately thirty-five thousand feet at the time. Using takedown moves that he learned at the police academy, Matt took the individual to the floor and announced that he was a police officer. Matt lamented that he did not have handcuffs, but one of the stewardesses brought him three flex ties that they bound together to restrain the screaming man. Two first class seats were cleared so that Matt and the screaming man could wait while the pilot declared an emergency. The plane was diverted to Salt Lake City, Utah and landed without incident. The Asian male was removed from the plane by Airport Police and the plane was again en route to its Los Angeles destination.

Once the disruptive passenger had been removed from the plane, Matt started back to his original seat to a rousing ovation from the other passengers on the plane.

Matt was totally unaware that his actions had been picked up by both FOX News and CNN and that he was being hailed as a hero. His plane had not landed yet when his parents saw the story that a police officer had saved the passengers on a flight from Cincinnati to Los Angeles from a mentally distraught passenger. His parents knew that it had to be Matt and were feeling very proud of him at this moment.

When the plane finally touched down and the passengers de-planed, Matt found two LAX airport cops waiting for him. They told him that a battery of media cameras were waiting for him in the passenger waiting area and that, if he wanted, they would take him out through a passageway not accessible to the public. Matt had no experience with handling the media and was happy to just sneak out of the airport.

Matt quietly rented a car while the Airport police retrieved his baggage for him and he now understood the respect cops will give to each other inconsequential of the distance they are apart.

Matt drove home feeling really tired from the long flight and the events of the day, but felt a sense of accomplishment that the training he was getting had potentially saved his and others lives. When he walked into what used to be his home, his parents were still awake and waiting for him. His mother ran up and hugged him and then his father told him that they had seen the story on the news and how proud they were to have him as their son. All Matt wanted right now was his bed and his mother's home cooking.

On Christmas morning Matt awoke with an energy he had not felt since his pre-teens. He ran down the steps to the smell of coffee and breakfast and his parents seated at the kitchen table. His mother had prepared his favorite blueberry waffle with warm maple syrup and what looked to be a whole pound of bacon. He ate slowly, savoring each bite, and enjoyed the home he grew up in. He laughed when he said that the only thing he missed about LA, other than them, was warm weather. He told them about leaving Cincinnati where the temp was twenty-two degrees.

The family took their cups of coffee and moved to the living room where the fully decorated for the Christmas holiday had been set up... Matt pulled an envelope out of his rear pocket and handed it to his mom. She opened it to find the two tickets for the cruise and handed them to his dad to inspect. Matt knew that his parents had to forgo many vacations to pay for his education, and hoped that they would be able to take them now that he was no longer a burden.

His parents wanted to know every minute of his experience as a police officer, but Matt knew there were things he really should not tell them. He told them about his two weeks on the street, leaving out the shotgun story. He told them about forming a study group with his classmates and the camaraderie that the recruits were forming and how much he was looking toward graduation to the street.

Matt and his dad sat in the family room and watched the football games on television while mom worked in the kitchen making Christmas dinner.

The next morning Matt picked up the phone and called the detective who had connected him with the hypnotist to tell him that an arrest had been made that would not have happened were it not for the information that Dr. No had elicited. He also told the detective that he was now halfway through the police academy and thanked him profusely. When Matt hung up the phone, the homicide dick had a big smile on his face and his colleagues did not have a clue as to why.

***

Matt returned to Cincinnati with a renewed sense of resolve. He wanted the academy to be over so that his parents would be able to see what their sacrifices and support had accomplished for him.

All of the eating and lounging created a minor problem for his first run since returning. The instructor was running along side of Matt yelling at him to pick up the pace. Matt had only minutes to shower and get into his recruit uniform before the classroom door would be locked and he would have to sit out in the hallway until the next break. At least no one had heard about the incident on the flight to LA or they were not asking about it.

The days toward graduation were going by very quickly. The only time that the recruits were able to leave the classroom was for the defensive driving training that was conducted in the parking lot of a former multi-screen movie theatre.

It was a Tuesday morning in Cincinnati and there was snow on the ground as Matt drove toward Spinney Field for class. He had slept in and did not get to drink his morning coffee or turn on the news.

The radio was turned to a station which had news on the half-hour and the lead story was that a Cincinnati cop had been seriously injured in the early morning hours. The report said the cop was dragged alongside a car for several blocks before falling off and being struck by a car. The officer's condition was unknown but the injuries were reported to be life threatening. When Matt walked in the entrance of the academy, he saw that the staff looked like zombies going about their tasks with no energy at all. Something was very wrong.

The recruits morning run had been cancelled and they were directed to report to the classroom. The commander walked into the room with his head down and told the recruits that the officer had died as a result of the injuries he suffered in the incident. The Lieutenant also told the recruits that the officer had killed the driver of the car dragging him with a single shot to the head. The dead driver was a thirteen year old boy who had taken the car without his parents' permission.

The recruits would be providing an honor guard for the funeral to be held at St. Peter and Chains in downtown Cincinnati. They would be forming two lines up the steps leading to the church prior to the arrival of the hearse carrying the body of the thirty-two old officer. They would receive an order to stand at attention as soon as the casket was removed from the hearse from a commander at the church and they were to salute until the casket passed them, so they would be dropping the salute in twos, one on each side. They would repeat this at the conclusion of the service and then would be transported to the burial site to form a second line for the casket to pass. The Lieutenant reminded them that this would be their opportunity to honor a fallen brother and that they needed to be crisp and in time with each other. They practiced the maneuver several times that morning.

On the morning of the funeral, the recruits met at the academy and were transported by van to the church. Many had gone to the funeral home the night before, in an effort to pay their respects to the family of the fallen officer. The area around the church was chaos. The church held over one thousand people and there was an overflow out into the streets of downtown which had all been shut down. Matt saw marked police cars from Kentucky, Indiana, Michigan, Tennessee, West Virginia and Illinois parked along the streets leading up to the church. The recruits were positioned in two lines with each recruit directly in line with their counterpart on the other side of the steps.

The hearse pulled up in front of the church and an Assistant Police Chief ordered everyone to attention. That included the hundreds of uniformed cops from other police agencies who followed the command, as if it was given by one of their own bosses. As the casket passed two aligned recruits, each crisply dropped their salute as if on cue. Their timing was absolutely perfect. Once the casket went into the church, the recruits went back to the vans that delivered them to get warm until the service was over. Television news vans were everywhere imaginable and the service was being aired live by a local station. The recruits were given a five minute warning that the service was about to end and regrouped on the steps for the exit of the casket. The recruits once again perfectly executed their assignments.

News reports would later say that the funeral procession made up of marked police units with only their overhead lights flashing extended more than three miles in a silent tribute to a fallen officer. Matt was in awe as he saw the number of people who had stood on the funeral route waving flags and paying their respects to a person they had never met. He was especially moved when he saw a boy, who looked four years old, holding his mother's hand and holding a small flag in his other hand on this icy cold day in Cincinnati.

At the end of the graveside service, police communications operator was heard on a loud speaker calling for car 5308, the call sign that the fallen officer used that night. The dispatcher made multiple requests for the officer to respond and then, in a monotone voice, announced that 5308 was 27 (the police signal for out of service) and may God rest his soul. Matt could see tears flowing from the lines of cops that surrounded the burial site and felt himself welling up inside for a man he had never met.

The officer was buried with full honors and the flag which had draped the casket was folded and handed to the officer's mother. It was a sad day in Cincinnati, Ohio.

The next day the classroom was unusually somber and quiet. The morning session started with a moment of silence for the officer's family and then the instructors used the tragedy as a teachable moment.

The officer had pulled his cruiser into the parking lot of a twenty-four hour convenience store. As the officer was leaving the store, he saw a male behind the wheel of a car who could barely see over the steering wheel. The officer told the male behind the wheel to turn off the car's engine, but the driver refused. The officer reached into the car to remove the key from the ignition when the driver put the car in gear and drove out of the parking lot. The officer's arm was caught in the steering wheel and he was dragged down the road. The officer was able to draw his gun and had fired one shot which entered the left side of the driver's head. The officer then apparently freed himself of the steering wheel and fell onto the street where he was struck by another vehicle.

The driver of the car drove it to his house and collapsed into his mother's arms and died. He turned out to be thirteen years old. The recruits were warned that reaching inside a car can have a deadly outcome.

The study group was meeting more and more often in order to prepare for the state test which was now less than two weeks away. The recruits were told that the state allowed them to fail the test once and retake it, but that the Police Department only allowed the test to be taken once, so if anyone failed they would be fired by the city. The state would bring the test to the academy, administer and proctor it, and then leave without grading it. The police academy would be sent the scores in two to three days. Once the scores were in, the recruits would have one additional week of training where they would learn city laws and the policies of the police department and that they would take a second test on the last week of training. Those who passed both tests would move onto graduation and the class would need to choose their valedictorian who would speak to the attendees of the ceremony including the Police Chief and the Mayor of Cincinnati.

The class elected Matt to be their spokesman at the ceremony.

Hugs abounded as the scores from the test were posted in the classroom. All of the recruits had passed the state written test. When everyone passed the second test as well, the new police officers were set to graduate.

The graduation ceremony would be held at the Cincinnati Convention Center. All of the Cincinnati Police hierarchy would be in attendance, as would the Mayor and many of the elected officials of the city. Matt had worked hard to offer a presentation that showcased the work of the class as a team and to express the class' hopes for the future.

The new police officers were given their gun belts and their new uniforms in a private area of the Convention Center. The Police Chief would hand each graduate their badge and shake their hand to complete their training program. Parents and friends of the graduates filled the room as the class marched two by two into the room and sat in chairs at the front of the hall. They were told to stand at attention and be sworn in as Cincinnati cops by the Police Chief, who welcomed them into the world of professional law enforcement. The Chief told the people in attendance that they were looking at the future of law enforcement in Cincinnati and that the future was looking very good.

Matt had not had much experience in public speaking, but was told by the class in the dressing area that he would perform admirably. Matt walked to the microphone and told the group that the people in the audience were truly the ones who were responsible for the success of this class. The first group Matt acknowledged were the friends and family of these recruits because, without the support of parents, spouses, significant others and friends, none of the recruits would be standing before them today. He then told the people in the room to give themselves a round of applause. He next thanked the instructors at the police academy because they always made themselves available to answer a question or offer any assistance possible to each of the recruits. He then asked that the instructors receive a round of applause for their efforts. Last, Matt complimented the recruits on their work ethic and dedication to each other to help each other succeed.

The ceremony ended with the Mayor wishing the recruits success in their career and telling them how much they were appreciated by the residents of Cincinnati.

As with almost all graduations, the new cops threw their white hats into the air in celebration.

CHAPTER THIRTEEN

Because Matt's parents were in the city specifically for Matt's graduation ceremony, Matt chose to skip the graduation party the recruits had scheduled. All of the recruits had kicked in fifty dollars and they used the money to rent a small ballroom at the downtown Westin Hotel. The graduation was held on Friday evening and the recruits would have Saturday off before going to their new assignments on Sunday. Sunday is the first of the work week for Cincinnati cops.

Matt's parents took him to the Precinct restaurant, which is one of the most exclusive in downtown, for dinner to celebrate and then they went down to the riverfront to enjoy the new park and area. Matt was now wearing his 9mm Smith and Wesson handgun concealed under his blazer and his new badge and identification card were in his rear pocket.

After a long day and night, Matt walked his parents back to their hotel and told them he would see them in the morning for breakfast. They would be flying back home to LA in the early afternoon. It was a tearful goodbye as his parents told him how proud of him they were and to make sure he stayed in contact with them.

Matt lounged around on Saturday night wondering what he had missed at the party and feeling bad that he had not even made an appearance, but realized that his family was more important than a party, even if it was the acknowledgement that he was now a police officer.

Matt was assigned to District One on first shift. District One covers the central business district as well as two of the toughest areas of the city, that being Over the Rhine and the West End. Matt's Field Training Officer would be a man named Bill O'Donnell.

Matt reported to work and parked in the employee lot. This is the same place as when he went to the oral interview on his first trip. Not having been given the code, Matt was unable to enter through the rear door and had to walk around the building and enter through the public entrance. He made a mental not to get the access code first thing.

Everyone in the briefing was talking about two cops from the recruit class that had graduated only two days ago had been fired for Conduct Unbecoming an Officer (called CUBO by cops). At a party after the graduation the two apparently got very drunk and got completely naked in the hotel ballroom. One of the staff was walking by and saw it and the police were called. Matt thanked God his parents had been in town and he did not attend.

Bill O'Donnell was a sixteen year veteran of the police department who had a reputation for his aggressiveness and being a high achiever and would be Matt's FTO. After briefing was over and they had gotten their radio designation, which was 1106, O'Donnell got into the driver's seat and Matt in the passenger side. O'Donnell told Matt that Matt would be with him for four weeks, then transfer to a second FTO for four weeks, then to a third, then come back to him for the final four weeks of the program. O'Donnell told Matt that Matt would have to earn the right to do anything as a police officer. He said Matt would not get to drive until he earned that privilege by following orders and proving his worth as a cop.

O'Donnell told Matt that his job as the passenger in the car was to handle the police radio, operate the siren should that be necessary and to tell the driver whether or not traffic on the right was clear if they needed to blow through an intersection on an emergency run. Matt would also be responsible for logging on the activity sheet the time they got dispatched, the time they arrived, the time they left, and the address and nature of the radio run.

O'Donnell told Matt that there are three types of cops: Pro active cops who search to find problems and resolve them quickly; Reactive cops who don't do anything they have to; and Rainbow, which he explained is a bread which had a commercial calling itself "the eight hour loaf." O'Donnell said only Matt would determine which category he wanted to fall into.

The very first thing the two cops did was drive into a White Castle and pick up two coffees. At a little after ten am, 1106 and two other cars were sent to 1214 Vine Street in Over the Rhine. The dispatcher told the responding that a woman had called 9-1-1 and was screaming uncontrollably and that nothing she said was understandable. The caller lived in Apartment 4b at that address. The three police cars entered the driveway of the apartment complex together, all with their overhead lights flashing. The other two units were one person cars and the four cops entered the building and went up one set of steps to the first landing. O'Donnell let out a gasp when he looked up toward the second landing because he saw the torso of a female whose head was missing. The four cops all drew their guns and went to Apartment 4b to talk to the complainant who told them that was the woman who lived with her husband Apartment 6b. When no one would come to the door one officer kicked the door open and they began searching the apartment. When the officers walked into the bedroom of the apartment, they saw a woman's head positioned perfectly on the pillow. Being that there was no one else in the apartment, they backed out the same way that they had entered and called for a supervisor and the homicide unit. More police units began arriving and checking out the scene. One officer, who had more than enough time on the job to retire walked over to Matt and told him that Matt's next twenty-five years would be a breeze because he had now seen it all.

Matt was looking at the old cop with a dazed look on his face when O'Donnell yelled at him to get his head out of his ass and get the crime scene tape from the trunk of the police car. The two cops used the tape to cordon off an area so the investigators could have a secure space for their work. About this time a marked police car pulled up to the scene and a Lieutenant got out of his car and began screaming at the group of cops just standing around to go find some police work to do or there was going to be hell to pay. Cops were suddenly scrambling to get back into their cruisers and get out of there. The Lt. told Matt and O'Donnell to remain at the scene until they were either relieved or the crime scene tape was taken down.

Matt was approached by one of the homicide guys and asked if Matt had seen anyone touch the torso in the hallway or the head that was on the pillow. The homicide dick looked relieved when Matt told him no one had tampered with the scene and told Matt that cops can really be some stupid people at times.

O'Donnell told Matt that he needed to quit acting like a spectator at a crime scene and just do his job. He told Matt that every experience was a learning opportunity. They were kept on the scene for about two more hours when two more cops arrived to relieve them. They grabbed a quick lunch at a drive-thru and went on about patrolling their beat. They watched a guy in a Porsche run a red light and O'Donnell watched Matt write the citation and made him change a few minor things that he missed. The two spent the last forty-five minutes before the end of shift discussing the events of the day.

Matt was told that he did fine at the homicide scene until he started listening to what other cops had to say instead of doing what he was supposed to. The traffic ticket was not completely filled out which could result in it being tossed in court. Matt had listed the nature of the call to Vine Street as a screaming woman and O'Donnell changed that to unknown trouble. O'Donnell told Matt that he didn't do too badly for a first day on the street.

At the start of the FTO program, Matt was provided the daily and weekly forms that needed to be completed by his trainer, and Matt would be responsible for keeping them through the changes in trainers so that his first FTO could sign off on him at the end of the sixteen weeks. Each task that Matt performed during a shift was scored on a seven point scale, with one being dismal and seven being perfect. His scores were expected to show improvement each and every week. If a listed task was not performed on a shift, that task would not be scored. The FTO would fill out a narrative on what thing(s) the recruit could have done better to help him or her improve their performance.

O'Donnell hammered home the fact that not all of Matt's working days would be action packed, but that every day presented dangers that Matt would have to be prepared to face.

With each passing shift Matt became more and more comfortable under the direction of O'Donnell. Matt would read the narrative that O'Donnell would write next to each task performed that would tell him what things he needed to improve to raise the score the next time. Matt was receiving positive reinforcement for the things he did right and constructive criticism for the areas that needed improvement. This was truly a learning experience for Matt.

At the end of the phase one of the FTO program O'Donnell told Matt he looked forward to seeing big changes in Matt's skill level when he would see Matt again in eight weeks. Matt would have three days off and then would start the midnight shift with his second trainer.

CHAPTER FOURTEEN

Matt arrived at the District for his first midnight shift. His new FTO was an officer named Darius Williams, a four year veteran of the department. Williams had played college basketball at the University of Dayton and had his degree in clinical psychology. Williams was known for his relaxed demeanor and being very low key, which many wrongly took as being a sign of weakness and paid the price for their mistake.

The two officers got into the police car after briefing and, as soon as Williams started the car, Matt rolled the passenger window down. When Williams quizzed Matt as to why he would do that in twenty degree weather, Matt told him that it was something Matt learned in his ride-a-long so that he could hear the sounds of the street outside the car. The two pulled out of the parking lot with their windows cracked open and the heater on full blast to start their shift. Their first shift together was pretty uneventful and the daily checklist was fairly easy for Williams to complete.

The next night Williams let Matt drive the cruiser for the first time. They were casually driving down a four lane street with no traffic when Williams glanced over at the speedometer and noticed that Matt was traveling just over fifty miles per hour in a thirty five mile per hour zone. Williams asked Matt if he had missed a radio call and when Matt told him that there was no call, Williams ordered him to pull the police car to the curb and shut it off. Williams told Matt that there was no excuse for him to violate the speed laws of the State of Ohio and ordered him out of the driver's seat until he learned how to operate a police car in a safe manner. Matt felt that he had let his FTO down. The fauxpax was discussed at length at the end of shift evaluation and Matt apologized to Williams for the error. It would not happen again.

Matt reported for his third midnight shift and the briefing was mundane because not a lot had occurred in the District over the past sixteen hours. Matt and his partner got into the cruiser to start their shift and Williams told Matt that he was progressing nicely in his training program. They patrolled the streets of their beat and checked the businesses that were closed to locate any unusual activity. After almost two hours of patrol they had yet to receive a radio and it looked like it was going to be a peaceful shift. Matt was still having difficulty adjusting his sleep habits because the noise of the daytime hustle and bustle of downtown made it difficult to get the proper sleep.

The dispatcher advised Car 1301 that they needed to Signal Two immediately and see the Captain. Signal Two is a code that tells officers to respond back to the Police District. When they arrived at the District, the desk officer told Williams that the Captain wanted to see Matt in his office alone. The two officers looked at each other quizzically and Matt walked to the Captain's door and knocked.

The Captain told Matt to have a seat and Matt became really nervous that he had done something wrong. The Captain walked around his desk and sat on the very edge near Matt's chair and told Matt that he had just gotten off the phone with the Los Angeles Police who told him that Matt's father was missing from the cruise ship and no one had been able to find him. He told Matt that his mother was being flown back to her home in LA and that the Captain had called in some favors. The FBI would be sending a team to the cruise ship and Matt needed to go to his apartment and pick up some clothes then drive his car to Wright Patterson Air Force Base where both he and his car would be flown to San Diego and Matt could drive to his mother's from there. The Captain said that a marked Ohio Highway Patrol unit would be waiting for him on the ramp to Interstate 75 to escort him to the exit for the Air Force base. He told Matt to turn on his emergency flashers so the trooper would know it was him. The Captain then gave Matt a business card and wrote his city issued cell phone number on it and told Matt that if he needed anything, night or day, to call him because Matt was a member of the Cincinnati Police family.

Matt rushed out the door of the District without even telling his partner what had happened. His mind was racing at a mile a minute and the fear was welling up inside him. After Matt went home and threw some clothing into a piece of luggage, he drove to the entrance ramp, saw the state vehicle and turned on his flashers. The trooper immediately activated the overhead lights and the siren on the patrol car. What should have a forty-five minute drive minute drive from Cincinnati been to just north of Dayton actually took twenty-six minutes.

Matt drove to the main gate at the Air Force base and was stopped by an officer at the gate. Matt told the officer that a plane was waiting for him and the officer immediately walked into the gatehouse to make a call. In what appeared to be seconds, two marked base police cars with their overhead lights flashing and sirens blaring, pulled up at the gate and told Matt that they would escort him to the tarmac and lead him directly to the plane.

Matt pulled up the rear of the plane which had its ramp down and ready. Matt was told by one of the crew members to get out of his car so that it could be driven up the ramp and into the plane. Matt walked up the ramp and into the cargo plane as the ramp was lifted to close.

The crew member told Matt he could either strap himself into the seats along the wall of the plane or seatbelt himself into the car for the flight which would take about six hours because the cargo plane could not reach the speeds of a passenger airline.

When the plane touched down at the San Diego airbase, his car was driven down the ramp and onto the tarmac, and the crew wished him well. Matt left the base and drove as fast and safely as he could to his parent's house in LA.

When he got there his mother met him at the door. Her face was swollen as she told Matt that she and his dad had just finished their dinner on the ship and that his dad went for a walk. After almost two hours of not seeing him, she reported him missing to a steward who instituted a ship-wide search that turned up nothing. The steward told her to go back to their cabin and the crew would keep looking. Mom told Matt that, since the ship was in international waters, multiple countries were providing assistance in the search, without success. She told him that after one and one-half days of searching, she was taken by helicopter to an airport and flown home. She told the crew early on that her son was a policeman and said that Los Angeles Police were waiting for her at the airport and brought her home and had been back to check on her telling her that Matt was on a plane to be with her. She told Matt that she had not slept in almost two days and was glad he was now there with her.

A United States Coast Guard cutter helping in the search found the body floating in the Pacific Ocean the next day. The coroner subsequently ruled that the man died from drowning, but there was no evidence to indicate how or even where Matt's dad had fallen off the ship.

Matt called the District One Captain and relayed the information that he knew at that point. The Captain told him to take the time he needed to get the affairs in California in order and that his job was secure. They would work out his training when he returned.

Matt's mother was now under a doctor's care for a mental breakdown and Matt was not doing much better. He was receiving calls on his cell phone from the people he attended the academy with as well as instructors and his FTO's asking if there was anything he needed, and he was thankful for the support the other cops offered him.

The body of Matt's father was released to the funeral home by the LA Coroner, but Matt was told that the damage done by the Pacific Ocean made it impossible to have an open casket. Matt almost had to carry his mother into the funeral home because she was so distraught and dysfunctional. Once inside, the first thing the two mourners saw was a large wreath with a card from the Fraternal Order of Police Queen City Lodge 69.

It had now been weeks since Matt had left Cincinnati and his mother was not improving. Deep down Matt knew that his concentrating on his mother kept him from thinking about the fact that his parents would not have been on that cruise ship and his father would still be alive had he not bought them the tickets.

***

It had been a little over three months since Matt Miles had returned to Los Angeles after his father had died tragically while on a cruise. The FBI had conducted an investigation and, after interviewing the staff and passengers, had determined that there was no evidence to conclude that the death was anything other than a tragic accident.

Matt had watched his mother deteriorate both physically and mentally since the death. She had stopped going to the doctor and now refused to eat. She was now becoming frail and weak and slept on the couch in the living room because she refused to even enter the bedroom she had shared for so long with her beloved husband. Matt would be awakened from his sleep by the loud crying of his mother and the crying appeared to be worsening with each passing day. She refused his requests to seek medical help with her physical and mental condition. She was forced to quit her job that she loved due to her uncontrollable mood changes, which, in turn, caused a deeper depression.

Matt had even tried getting his mother out of the house by taking her to restaurants that his family had never gone to in an effort to get her to eat. They would order their food and, when it arrived at the table, Matt's mother would start crying uncontrollably disrupting the other patrons. Matt would pay for the food that was not eaten and take his mother home. He was beginning to get really scared for her health and welfare.

Matt finally decided to sit his mother down and talk about what she was going through. He was shocked when she told him that she had lost all will to live and just wanted to be reunited with her husband.

Matt went up to his bedroom and was lying on the bed when he remembered something that he had learned at the Police Academy. Ohio has a law that allows a police officer to involuntarily commit a person to a mental institution for a maximum of seventy-two hours if that person presents a danger to themselves or to others. Matt went over to his computer and did a search of California law to see if there was anything similar. He found that California has the same provision in their statutes. Now he had a decision to make. Matt agonized over his decision, as he had to weigh the risk of alienating his mother against the very real possibility that her depression would end in suicide.

After what seemed like an eternity, Matt walked over to the telephone and dialed the Los Angeles Police Communication Center. He did not want to hear sirens and have multiple police cars pulling up in front of his house, so he chose his words to the operator very carefully. Matt told the female operator that he needed to talk to a police officer about a mentally ill woman at his residence who was unarmed and non-violent. The operator told Matt that a police officer would be dispatched. He knew that the call would be a low priority and he would probably have to wait awhile.

Matt took his cup of coffee and sat on the porch awaiting the arrival of the police. After forty-five minutes of waiting, Matt saw a marked cruiser pull up in front of his house. A female police officer exited the passenger side of the marked unit and a male exited the driver's door. They walked up the sidewalk leading to the house and Matt met them on the porch. Matt showed the officers his Cincinnati badge and told them that he needed a favor from them. He explained the situation and told them he wanted to have his mother involuntarily committed.

The female officer, a fifteen year veteran of LAPD, gave Matt a strange look and told him that she had never been asked to do that before and was really uncomfortable making that kind of decision. The male half of the team suggested that they call for a supervisor and let him make the decision. The female made the radio request for a supervisor to respond.

The three stood on the porch and chatted for the next twenty-five minutes until a second marked police car arrived. The Sergeant, who had twenty-one years on the job, got out of his vehicle and walked up onto the porch. The two LA cops explained what Matt had asked them to do and that Matt was also a cop from Cincinnati, Ohio.

Matt took the Sergeant through the death of his father and the events that followed. When he was done the Sergeant told Matt he wanted to talk with Matt's mother and would then make a decision. The four walked into the house where Matt's mother was sitting in a chair in the living room staring blankly at the wall. The Sergeant told his two officers to take Matt out onto the porch and wait for him.

The Sergeant immediately noticed that the woman's eyes were sunken and her body looked extremely frail. He politely introduced himself to her and asked if he could chat with her. She simply nodded and continued to stare blankly out into space. The Sergeant asked what had happened to her husband and the woman immediately broke into a crying jag that Matt could hear from the porch. Matt had to fight off an urge to go running back into the house to protect his mother because he knew the Sergeant was simply trying to conduct an assessment.

Matt's mother told the Sergeant about the cruise accident and that she had lost all interest in life and just wanted to join her husband. The Sergeant thanked her for talking and walked back out onto the porch where he called for an ambulance to come to the house. The Sergeant ordered the female to ride in the ambulance with Matt's mom and to sign the seventy-two hour mental health hold. The Sergeant then told Matt to drive to UCLA Medical Center so he could be with his mother when she arrived at the hospital.

Minutes later an ambulance arrived and paramedics put Matt's mother on a gurney to be transported to the hospital. Matt was a bit surprised that his mother offered no resistance at all.

Matt was able to follow behind the ambulance and the police car because the trip did not require the use of lights and siren. When they arrived at the hospital, Matt's mom was taken into the Emergency Room while the female officer signed the forms necessary for the hold. The doctor in the ER ordered a feeding tube to be inserted so that Mrs. Miles could receive nutrients that she desperately needed. As she was taken to the Psychiatric Unit, Matt was able to kiss his mother and tell her how much he loved her. Matt drove home feeling sick about what he had to do, but knew that he had done the right thing.

Matt was floating on air as he drove back to his house. When he arrived he saw the postman standing at the front door. The letter carrier had just turned to leave when Matt approached and the carrier told Matt that he needed his signature on a certified letter. The letter was on City of Cincinnati letterhead and was signed by the Police Chief informing Matt that, due to the length of his absence, the City had made the decision that Matt has resigned his position as a Police Officer and that Matt needed to turn in his badge, identification and all equipment within five days of his receipt of the letter.

Matt found himself in a quandary because he had come to love his job and living in Cincinnati, but family was his first priority hands down. Matt walked into the house and called the Captain of District One on the phone. He told the Captain of the letter and that he would send his weapon, badge and identification via overnight shipment with Federal Express. He told the Captain that he would call the manager of his apartment and that he would have the manager allow a police officer access to his uniforms, gun belt and radio that were in his bedroom closet.

The Captain thanked Matt for his quick response and told Matt that the City had a policy of allowing officers who resigned in good stead to re-apply within one year of their termination date and, if an opening exists, he would be re-hired without having to go through the testing or police academy. The Captain wished him well in whatever the future would hold for Matt and told him that if he ever needed a recommendation to use the Captain's name.

Once again, Matt was not happy with the decision he made, but knew in his heart that he had made the correct choice.

***

It was not until the next morning when the Psychiatrist who had been assigned to assess Mrs. Miles was able to talk to her for the first time. The doctor really did not like LA cops and hated it when they forced people to be evaluated. He figured he could have this woman out the door in fifteen minutes after reading the form signed by the stupid cop.

He walked into the room and introduced himself to the patient, who was staring blankly at the wall. He noticed the feeding tube that had been inserted and also took notice of how frail and weak the woman appeared. Since the commitment form identified this woman's son as a police officer in Cincinnati, Ohio, the doctor opened the conversation with how her son had become a cop there. Mrs. Miles smiled meekly and was very lucid in her discussion about her son. The doctor knew his preliminary opinion that the LA cops overreacted was accurate until Mrs. Miles talked about the death of her husband. She went into a crying jag and told the shrink that she needed to join her husband of twenty-five years and that life was no longer worth living. The doctor suddenly realized that he had a problem on his hands and that this woman needed to be treated immediately.

At the end of the interview the doctor went back to his office and called Matt. He told Matt that his mother was going to be kept at the hospital and treated for her depression. He told Matt that a grief counselor would be working with his mother as well and that he could not give a time frame on when she would be released. Matt thanked the doctor and suddenly felt good about making the difficult decision to commit her. Matt made a daily ritual of visiting her at the hospital and saw almost immediate improvement in both her physical and mental state. In his most recent visit Matt met with the doctor managing his mother's care and was told she would be ready to come home in a couple of weeks.

CHAPTER FIFTEEN

Matt was sleeping soundly when he was awakened by the telephone. It was the lead doctor who called to tell him that he could come and pick up his mother that afternoon.

As Matt wandered into the kitchen to make coffee, he looked around the spacious house and all he saw was sadness. He needed to find a way to get his mother out of this house as part of her return to normalcy. Matt needed to conjure up a way to get his mother to move to Cincinnati with him and restart her life in a new place.

She would never have to worry about money issues because Matt's father had taken out a one million dollar life insurance policy with a double indemnity clause for accidental death, giving her two million dollars in the bank. Matt would have to work out the kinks of his mother staying with him in his studio apartment until he could get her settled, but that problem would work itself out. Matt had no clue whether he would be able to get his job back, but decided Cincinnati was the place that he wanted to be.

Matt drove slowly to the hospital formulating a plan that he hoped his mother would buy into. He would take her out for a dinner at a new Irish Pub he had seen and hope that the memories of her English heritage would keep her mood upbeat. Once at the hospital, Matt waited patiently until a nurse brought out his mother in a wheelchair. He led the way back to the car where both helped his mother into the passenger seat and they had a quiet drive home.

That evening Matt took his mother to a restaurant called Houligan's where the staff spoke in brogue and the setting was straight out of Ireland. They sat quietly in a booth and worked on their brisket and cabbage meals when Matt softly broke the concept of his mother moving out of the house and relocating to Cincinnati. He told her that California had nothing left to offer her and that she would love the sights and sounds of Cincy. The look on her face appeared puzzled at first and Matt thought his timing may well have been wrong but, after a few moments of thought, his mother nodded her head in agreement and the thought of a new life brought a small smile to her face.

They returned to the house and, although his mother still slept on the couch, she slept through the night without incident.

Matt contacted real estate agents to come out and list the house. He and his mom began packing the things that she would want to take with her and Matt was surprised that she had no fear of entering the bedroom that had caused so much consternation since his dad's death. With the house now up for sale, Matt and his mother began planning their move to Ohio.

***

Back in Cincinnati, the Captain of District One sat at his desk looking at an open FedEx box that contained the badge, identification and gun of Matthew Miles with sadness. It was just an unfortunate chain of events that forced the resignation and Cincinnati had lost a potential great officer. All the Captain could do is wish this young man well and hope that he would have a successful career and life.

Matt and his mother sat in the living room discussing how they were going to make the transition to Cincinnati. Matt suggested that they make the drive to Cincinnati a vacation and visit some of the historic areas on the way. She had never seen the Grand Canyon or the badlands of Wyoming and they might even stop in Las Vegas on the way. Matt told his mother that there was not much need to keep all of the furnishings in the home and to go through the house and decide what she wanted to have moved there. They would place them in a storage facility while they searched for a new place for her. Matt said she could fly back to California for the house closing and that he loved the thought of having her nearby to share in his life.

Within a week they started the trek toward Cincinnati. As Matt promised, it was a leisurely ride that took eight days to complete. His mother's mood was upbeat and she was beginning to return to the vivacious person he knew and loved. They were even able to talk about Matt's dad without her breaking down.

Once back in Cincinnati, Matt needed to begin the process of trying to return to employment with the City. He went to the City Human Relations Department and filed a new application for the position of police officer. He attached a letter requesting reinstatement as he was told to do by the District One commander. The personnel officer told him that the application would be forwarded directly to the Police Chief for evaluation. All that Matt could do now was wait.

The living arrangements in the studio apartment presented some challenges, as it was not conducive to a mother and son living arrangement. Matt went out and purchased a partition to separate the bed area from the living room in order to provide his mother some level of privacy, and he was back to sleeping on the air mattress he had bought when he first moved in.

They would spend the days riding around Cincinnati looking at houses and apartments that his mother might enjoy. They look at the suburbs and tried to find something close to shopping and leisure. They had sold the family car before they left California, so they would need to get her a new one at some point in the very near future. She really seemed to enjoy the slower pace of life, as it was completely different than the helter-skelter world of LA.

Matt and his mom were enjoying breakfast when the telephone rang in the apartment. The caller was the Police Chief's secretary who told

Matt the Police Chief wanted to schedule an interview at the earliest possible convenience. Matt told the woman that he would be available whatever time was convenient for the Chief. They set a time of one-thirty that afternoon in the Chief's Office.

Matt pulled up to District One and was unsure whether he should park in the employee lot since he was no longer an employee. He decided to park on the opposite side of the street and entered through the public entrance for his meeting. He did not see anyone that he recognized at the front desk and told the desk officer that he was there for a meeting with the Police Chief. The deskman directed him to the elevator and that the Chief's Office was on the third floor.

Matt was clearly nervous as he sat outside the office of the Police Chief. He watched the secretary busily performing her job and worked on his breathing to try to reduce his level of anxiety. He watched the secretary answer the phone and then look up to tell him the Chief would see him now. Matt's only personal contact with the Chief had been at the graduation ceremony when the Chief handed him his badge and shook his hand.

The Police Chief's office was spacious but functional. The Chief shook Matt's hand and pointed toward a chair placed off center from the desk. Matt sat down in the chair making sure that his posture projected attentiveness. The Chief told Matt that he was aware of the tragedy that happened and hoped that his family was coping with it as well as can be expected.

The Chief wanted to know what brought Matt back to Cincinnati, rather than being with his family on the west coast. Matt explained that he had brought his mother back with him and that his mother was the only real family that he still had. Next the Chief wanted to know why Matt wanted to be rehired as a police officer and Matt went into great detail about the positive experiences the police department had given him and how much he loved the job.

Matt was shocked when the Chief got a scowl on his face and ordered Matt out of his office. Matt dutifully got out of his chair and was turning toward the door to leave as the Chief reached into his top left hand drawer. The Chief told Matt he would need this before he left and tossed him a black leather case. Matt opened the case and saw his police badge and identification and his smile literally lit up the room. Matt quietly closed the Chief's door and immediately saw the smile on the face of the secretary who was seated at her desk. She handed Matt his order to report to District One on the midnight shift Sunday night.

CHAPTER SIXTEEN

When Matt arrived at District for his first shift, cops lamented his bad luck in drawing his training officer greeted him. Liza Seemoan was a twelve-year veteran who the street cops called "bitchwitch" because she washed out more recruits than all of the other FTO's in the District combined. Seemoan is a five foot four inch woman who weighs one hundred and eighteen pounds and came to the Police Department with a Masters Degree in Police Administration and a fourth degree black belt in Tai kwon do. Her last job prior to joining the police department was as a bunny at the Cincinnati Playboy Club. It is easy to understand why male cops drooled over her. She was believed to have decked more cops than suspects in her career with the Department. Liza Seemoan became a legend when she made a traffic stop while working alone and found that the driver was wanted for putting his fiancé in the hospital after they had an argument. Seemoan ordered the driver out of the car and he punched her in the face, knocking her to the ground. She put out a call on her radio for assistance and police cars from Cincinnati and surrounding agencies rushed to her aid. As the second wave of screaming cruisers pulled up on the scene, the arriving cops were astounded to see male cops, with shotguns in their hands, sitting on their cruiser hoods watching Seemoan bounce the six foot four inch two hundred forty pound male around the parking lot like a tennis ball. The moron was a body builder, and the cops who tried to handcuff him had to interlock three sets of cuffs because his hands would not reach back far enough.

At the briefing, the Sergeant issued the beat assignments for the night. He welcomed Matt back to the Police Department and then wished all the cops a safe shift. Matt and his new FTO then walked out to the parking lot to start their shift. Seemoan tossed Matt the keys to the car and told him he needed to prove his worth to her or he would be selling typewriters like so many before him. Matt recalled vividly his first experience driving a police car and vowed that he would be cognizant of his speed at all times.

They were driving north on Vine Street in Over-the-Rhine when a description was broadcast of a purse-snatching suspect. The suspect was described as a male Hispanic approximately twenty years of age wearing a dirty white t-shirt and dark pants. As Matt turned west on Fifteenth Street, he saw a male fitting the description running west. He yelled to Seemoan who jumped out of the moving police vehicle to chase the suspect, forgetting to close the passenger door. Matt jammed the gas petal down and then slammed on the brakes to get the passenger door closed. He then activated the overhead lights to give chase turning south onto Race Street. He saw the suspect on the ground with Seemoan trying to handcuff him immediately as he made the turn. He jumped out of the cruiser and helped her secure the suspect. When they placed the suspect in the back of the police car, Seemoan demanded to know what took Matt so long. Matt looked at the lady cop and told her he would have been right there with her if she had thought to close the passenger door when she jumped out. Seemoan just smiled meekly and told him he had done well. They took the suspect back to the scene of the robbery and he was identified by the victim. The two cops turned the suspect over to the officers at the scene and returned to their beat. Seemoan marked the box Felony Arrest on their activity sheet and put them back in service with Police Communications.

The two officers were sitting at a red light at Liberty and Vine Street when Seemoan told Matt that he was expected to write one traffic citation per shift. Matt told her that he was unaware that Cincinnati had a quota system in place. Liza shot him a look intended to kill and said it was not a quota. If an officer works a whole shift and does not see any traffic violations, he has to be driving with his eyes closed. No sooner did those words come out when the car waiting next to them at the light stepped on the gas and blew through the red light. The car had four male occupants and Matt approached from the driver's side while Liza took a position behind the rear passenger door. Matt was reaching the driver's door when he heard his partner yell "GUN!," drew her weapon, and scrambled back to the passenger side of the cruiser. Matt backed up quickly and took a position behind the driver's door while Liza radioed for assistance. It seemed like only seconds had passed when four cruisers arrived with lights and sirens on. They ordered the occupants of the car out one at a time and had them lay flat on the pavement with their arms extended. When all four were out of the car, officers cuffed each and Matt and her partner went to the car to search for the gun. They recovered a loaded Tech9 semi-auto handgun from under the passenger seat. A warrant check found two others to be wanted felons so they arrested three of the four occupants and called for a tow truck to haul away the vehicle. They took the person closest to the gun to jail and the other wanted suspects were transported by other police units.

Matt did not have any experience driving into the Hamilton County Justice Center. He pulled up to a steel door with a microphone attached to a pole and pushed the button. A voice in the box asked, "Can I help you?" Matt looked at Seemoan who yelled, "Cincinnati Police with a prisoner." The steel door slowly opened. Liza told Matt to pull up to the next steel door and to stop. The door behind the cruiser slowly closed and then the door in front of them opened. Matt pulled into a parking space in the sally port and the officers got out of the car. Liza told Matt to open the trunk and walked to the back of the cruiser, unholstering her gun and placing it in the trunk. She told Matt to do the same. They then removed the prisoner and took him into the booking area of the Jail. They had to go into an interview room and complete the necessary paperwork to book the man into the Jail and then wait while jail officers searched the suspect. As the jail personnel emptied the suspect's pockets, a baggie of what appeared to be crack cocaine fell out, adding a new felony charge.

When they left the jail, Liza reminded Matt to open the car trunk so they could retrieve their firearms. She told Matt that, by placing them in the trunk of the police car, they would not forget and leave without them. Matt pulled the patrol car out of the parking area and waited for a steel door to open that allowed them to leave. Liza told Matt to drive to the White Castle on Central Parkway so they could get coffee and talk about what happened. Matt found himself in a quandary because the White Castle is in District Five and he did not want to get himself into any trouble. He also did not want to piss off his partner who was the one who would be evaluating him. He decided to ask her whether it was okay to cross the District boundaries without having a call. She just laughed and told him they were going to get along fine. They picked up their coffees and went to a parking lot back in District One to talk. Liza told him that she was impressed by his reaction time and the way that he handled himself and that the reason she had completed all of the arrest paperwork for expediency. She told Matt that he would be doing paperwork in the near future. The rest of the shift was uneventful.

Seemoan decided she wanted to drive the second night. They found out at briefing that the four people from the night before were gang-bangers Vine looking for trouble and they got an "attaboy" from the Sergeant. They no sooner pulled out of the lot when they received a radio run to respond to Thirteenth and Vine Street for a report of a naked man in the street. When they arrived Seemoan used the cruiser to block traffic traveling northbound on Street and the two officers walked through a large crowd of people who had congregated to watch. They saw a male in his forties running back and forth through a broken glass door. With each pass, the jaded glass was cutting deeper into the man's skin and he was bleeding profusely. The crowd screamed at the two cops to take some kind of action. Seemoan ordered Matt to get the beanbag shotgun out of the trunk of the cruiser and to make sure that he grabbed the correct shotgun. Cincinnati Police carry two shotguns in their trunk; one loaded with buckshot and the other with non-lethal beanbag rounds. The shotgun with the beanbags is marked with bright orange paint.

Matt ran to the cruiser and grabbed the beanbag shotgun as he was instructed. Seemoan ordered him to take the shot and knock the crazy man down. Matt fired and hit the man in the abdomen knocking the wind out of him, but he rose quickly and ran directly toward the officers. Matt tackled the suspect and Seemoan tried to grab onto him, but the blood and the fact there was nothing to grab onto made the job difficult. Seemoan fired her Taser and the man hit the ground just as paramedics from the fire department approached. With protective gloves on, the paramedics were able to hold the crazy guy down while the officers put the cuffs on. The man was then lifted onto a gurney and restrained with leather straps. He was transported to University Hospital and taken into the Psych Unit after being treated in the Emergency Room. Seemoan rode in the Rescue Unit while Matt followed behind. Matt completed a three-day mental hold on the individual to assure that he would be evaluated.

Their uniforms were covered with the subject's blood so they had to drive back to the District to change clothes. Matt did not have a spare uniform in his locker, but lived in the District so, after Liza changed her uniform, they drove to Matt's apartment and he ran up to change his while Liza waited in the car. He startled his mother when he entered the apartment covered in blood. He laughed and calmly told his mother it was not his. Matt made a commitment to always keep a complete uniform in his locker in the future. Luckily, the remainder of the evening was uneventful. Liza commented that Matt was beginning to be fun to work with.

Matt was experiencing problems with his daytime sleep because his mother was in the open space apartment at all times. His weariness was beginning to show and Seemoan commented about it when they got into the car for their third night shift.

After taking a mundane neighbor complaint on Pleasant Street, the two officers were patrolling the downtown business district when police communications put out a broadcast that a Kenton County, Kentucky deputy sheriff had put out an assistance call on the Suspension Bridge. Covington, Kentucky police had advised the deputy was attempting to make a DUI arrest and the subject was fighting him. Matt activated the overhead lights and siren and they rushed to the aid of a fellow officer. When they arrived they saw one marked Covington Police unit on the bridge with its lights flashing, but only saw one officer. The deputy was screaming that the Covington officer had tried to jump a barrier between the roadway and the walkway and had fallen into the Ohio River, more than one hundred feet below. The river was jet black and there was no visible sign of the officer anywhere. Seemoan called for the fire department amphibious vehicle and Kentucky officers requested water rescue from nearby Boone County, Kentucky.

A search went on throughout the night, and for days after, with no sign of the officer or his body. It was not until almost three months later that the officer's body was found.

After spending the shift walking the riverfront looking for the missing cop, Matt was feeling depressed on top of being tired. He was really looking forward to his upcoming three days off.

The last night shift ran really smooth and Matt and Liza were able to talk about the week they had experienced. Liza completed the weekly evaluation and they discussed the improvements Matt could make to be a more complete officer. They would return for four days of second shift.

CHAPTER SEVENTEEN

Matt took his mother out looking for a house to buy. Their house in LA still had not sold, but there was no rush for that to happen. Matt took his mom out to an area called Linwood, just on the eastern side of Cincinnati. There were several homes that she liked from the outside and she really liked how close the shopping area was. They had lunch in a restaurant that had been featured on the Food Channel and was renowned for their hamburgers. It was the first day that she had been able to just relax with her son and she was savoring every minute with him.

Matt took her to Ault Park and showed her the view of the River from the hillside. She could see the rolling hills of Northern Kentucky from her spot and the sun was out with bright blue skies. She was really glad she let Matt talk her into coming to Cincinnati.

Matt wrote down the phone numbers of the houses his mom really liked and would set appointments to see them on his days off. Matt and his mom also chatted about the possibility of finding her a part-time job just to keep her busy while she learned the area. She had experience as a secretary and she should be able to find employment relatively easily.

Matt's mom fixed him a nice dinner and they sat and watched television together all evening long. Matt no longer had much interest in television cop shows since he had experienced the real thing firsthand. His mom seemed to like the CBS show Big Brother and that was okay with Matt. Matt sort of expected his mom to ask him about all of the experiences he had so far, but was happy when she did not. The three off days went way to quick, but Matt would be able to sleep in the dark and that was a good thing.

Matt was ready to go back to work after the three days he spent bonding with his mother. She had made an offer on a house that she liked and they were awaiting the answer from the owners.

Matt was beginning to wonder about the information he had been given about Seemoan. She appeared to be cop who just wanted to do a good job and he was appreciative of the information she provided him.

They left the District and Liza wanted to drive. They had been out about an hour when a call came in for an auto accident with injuries on I-75 northbound just south of the Harrison Avenue exit. When they arrived they saw a car on its top in the center lane of the interstate and were told that the driver was still in the car. Seemoan went to the driver and determined that he had serious injuries and contacted police communications to dispatch Air Care, the medical helicopter that is housed at University Hospital. Calling out the helicopter meant that the complete interstate would need to be closed so that the chopper would have a place to land. The fire personnel had also arrived and were using the Jaws-of-Life to extricate the driver, who was a male in his fifties. The helicopter landed on the interstate while the firemen were still working to get the driver out of the car. Matt was amazed when a doctor, two nurses and two attendants jumped from the helicopter with gear and a gurney. As soon as the firemen opened the car, the doctor was there providing emergency medical attention and getting the man ready to be transported. The helicopter was airborne in a matter of minutes. In Cincinnati, the traffic section handles all serious crashes, so all the two cops had to do was keep the northbound interstate closed off to allow the traffic cops to do their thing. Matt saw the traffic guys bring out a laser-measuring device and track the original crash to a cement retaining wall that separates the north and southbound lanes. The interstate was closed for more than three hours during rush hour and the road was a mess.

When the two cops were told they could secure their post, Liza suggested that they try to eat before the evening madness started. She took him to a little hole in the wall that she told Matt had great sandwiches. Matt ordered a ham and beef double-decker while Liza had a tuna salad sandwich. When they went to leave, the cashier cut the price by half and wrote "POLICE" on the check. Both left a nice tip and thanked the waitress for the service.

Almost on cue, communications called with a run to Great American ballpark to meet an off-duty detail officer who had a prisoner. They pulled up in front of the stadium to see two officers struggling with the prisoner who was both intoxicated and agitated. When the prisoner saw the little red dot on his chest from the Taser, he relaxed and they were able to get him into the back of the cruiser. The prisoner told Matt that he had been "Tased" before and that, at the jail, the inmates had specific terms for it. They would tell each other they had "sat in the chair" referring to the electric chair, or that they had "rode the bull" referring to a ride on a mechanical bull. Matt just laughed and the guy was not a problem any longer. The off-duty officer had completed all of the necessary paperwork at the stadium, so all the two cops had to do was deposit him at the jail. The rest of the shift was quiet except for the one traffic ticket they wrote for a loud muffler.

Day two of second shift, which is two o'clock to twelve o'clock, started off with a bang. While still in roll call, they were given a radio run to 1216 Pendleton in Over the Rhine for a home invasion in progress. Matt activated the siren and lights and they were there in three minutes, after running out of the briefing room. Two other police units arrived at approximately the same time and the five officers went to the front door that was standing open. They heard moaning coming from inside the house and found two men in their twenties who had been shot. One appeared to have a life-threatening wound to the chest and the other had been shot in the arm. Neither wanted anything to do with the police and would not even talk to them. There were six other people in the house, including two young children. When they all were asked what had happened, none remembered anything. This was going to a tough one for the detectives, but Matt thought "better them than me."

Two other cops were told to remain at the scene and Matt and Liza were ordered back on patrol. Matt drove back down to the stadium area to have a police presence as the game let out and the patrons were walking back to their cars. They parked on the street and sat and watched people entering the bars and restaurants at the Banks as well as those preparing to leave in their cars. Matt was somewhat surprised that people actually waved to the cops sitting in their police vehicle like they were glad to have them there to protect them. When the crowd dwindled down, the two cops resumed riding around the downtown area trying to find something to get into. Liza told Matt that is what pro-active cops do.

When they passed the alley where Matt had witnessed the homicide, Matt stopped the car and told Liza the story about it. When he was finished, Liza said she had heard that a police applicant helped solve the case, but never knew who it was until now. Matt and Liza were developing a friendship as well as being partners.

As they passed Fountain Square, both officers heard the sounds of glass breaking. Matt turned down an alley just in time to see two males, who were obviously juveniles, running west away from them. He stomped on the gas petal and was on top of the two in seconds. This time, Seemoan waited until the police car was stopped before jumping out and closed the passenger door. Matt radioed that his partner was in foot pursuit and in less than two minutes the area was saturated with cops. Matt found his partner two blocks later, but the two juveniles were nowhere to be found. The two went back to the area where they heard the sound and found a car with the driver's window shattered and glass laying on the ground. While they were waiting for the registration of the owner to come back from communications, they were informed one of the suspects was in custody and the officers would be bringing him back to them. When the car arrived, Liza identified the suspect and took custody of him. They would have to take him to the Juvenile Detention Center, just northeast of the downtown area at 2020 Auburn Avenue. The kids in Cincinnati had decided that since 20 and 20 equals 40, that would be their name for the place. In Ohio, no matter what the offense, juveniles can only be charged with delinquency and, since the holding center has a limited capacity, only the most violent offenders are kept. The rest are released to the custody of a parent or guardian. The two officers got to put a checkmark for a felony arrest and a juvenile arrest, helping their statistics for the month. The two returned to patrol and wrote their obligatory one citation and that was their day.

***

Matt answered the phone in his apartment the next morning. It was the realtor who told him his mother's bid on the house had been rejected by the owner. Matt's mom had an interview for a secretarial position at Proctor and Gamble Company that afternoon, which was within walking distance of his apartment.

When Matt arrived at the District for his shift, he found a note in his bin telling him that he had been scheduled for his annual firearm proficiency test at the Police Firearm Training facility the following day. He was to report to the facility at two-thirty in the afternoon. Matt would need to tell Liza so they could go straight there after roll call.

Matt and Liza were detailed to the riverfront to stop a rash of purse snatching that had taken place in the late afternoons. They parked the police car near the Public Landing and walked the half mile area along the river. There were lots of people enjoying the serene setting of the river that the City had poured so much money into. Families having picnics, people resting in the warm sun, and groups of young males who appeared to be prowling for trouble. As soon as the groups would see the two cops walking, they would change their direction away from the cops. They walked through a tunnel that separates Yeatman's Cove from Sawyer Point when they heard a woman screaming for help. They ran to the woman who reported she had just been groped in her genital area by a white male who then inserted his finger into her vaginal cavity. That, in Ohio, constitutes rape.

Matt put out a description over the police radio while Liza took the report. As she was completing the report, Matt observed a man standing on the edge of a bridge over the Ohio River looking like he was preparing to jump. Matt yelled to Liza who turned just in time to see the man let go of his grip and fall the one hundred plus feet into the murky river. Liza screamed into her radio for the fire department duck and both officers ran to see if they could see the man in the water. Liza told Matt to return to the rape victim so that she could be transported to the hospital to be checked out. Moments later detectives from the Personal Crimes Unit arrived and took the victim with them. Matt went back to where Liza was and watched as the fireboat searched the Ohio River for the man. They were unable to find a body.

The two cops found a vendor selling hot dogs and brats. They stood against a rock wall and ate their sandwiches while watching the people enjoying the area. As darkness came, the two cops continued their efforts to prevent a crime from occurring by being very visible and vigilant. The waterfront gets extremely dark at night and the only sounds emanate from barges moving slowly on the river. Matt now understood why Cincinnati has a reputation as being one of the safest downtown areas in the United States. The more visible the presence of uniformed officers, the less opportunity for crime to be committed. The two moved over to Smale Park because that would be the most likely area for people to congregate in the late hours of the evening. People were quietly enjoying the water show and everyone looked like they were having fun. People walked over to the two officers and thanked them for their presence, which made Matt proud to be wearing the uniform.

Matt's final two weeks with Seemoan would be on day shift and he wanted to learn as much as he could from her. As Matt was walking to his car in the parking lot, he decided to stop and pick up his mom's favorite flavor of ice cream because it would provide an opportunity to discuss their living arrangements. The apartment was absolutely perfect for a single or a couple, but was not conducive to a mother and son because it offered no privacy.

When Matt left the police parking lot he decided to pick up a treat for his mom. He drove to a United Dairy Farmers, which is a regional convenience store chain that offers homemade ice cream products. UDF was started in the 1940's as a family run home delivery operation from a small location in the center of Cincinnati and developed into a chain of several hundred stores from Cincinnati to Columbus, Ohio. Its patriarch, Carl H. Lindner, Jr., began in the dairy and moved on to be the CEO of Chiquita Brands and American Financial and was a major donor of millions of dollars to charitable organizations.

Matt parked on the side of the building and left his white hat laying on the passenger seat since he was no longer required to wear it. He walked in the front door and smiled at the pretty young female clerk behind the counter. He went directly down the first aisle toward the freezer section and picked up a quart of ice cream. He moved back up the opposite end aisle to pay and go home. As he got in view of the counter, he saw a short male black subject pointing a gun at the clerk. Matt quietly put the ice cream on a shelf, drew his 40 caliber semi-automatic from the holster and stepped into the view of the robber. Cincinnati Police portable radios are equipped with a panic button feature. The button in encased in plastic so that cannot be activated my mistake. Matt pushed the panic button which sent a digital signal to the communication center. The only information which appeared on the dispatcher's screen was the number of the radio and to whom it is assigned. There was no gps which would tell them where Matt actually was. The dispatcher activated a set of tones which automatically opens the frequencies of all of the police agencies surrounding Cincinnati, including northern Kentucky and southeastern Indiana advising that an off-duty police officer needed assistance, but that his location was unknown. The broadcast told officers that Matt had just left District One Police Headquarters and put out a description and the license number of his Mustang. An intense search of the Greater Cincinnati area began immediately. A District One car was passing the UDF store and saw Matt's Mustang parked along the side of the building. He radioed the information and police cars from multiple districts started screaming toward that location.

Meanwhile, inside the store Matt ordered the suspect to drop the weapon. The suspect responded that Matt should drop his gun or that he would shoot the clerk. Without hesitation, Matt told the robber to go ahead and shoot the clerk and that before the clerk dropped to the floor, the suspect would be dead from a bullet to the head. They both stood motionless for what appeared to be an eternity. Matt told the guy that if the weapon moved in any direction toward him, or he shot the clerk, that Matt would put one bullet into the side of the man's head and he would be dead before the clerk hit the ground. Deciding he could not win, the robber placed the gun on the counter and stepped back.

Police cars from everywhere were screaming into the parking lot with their beacon lights on and sirens squealing. A twenty-four year old policeman from neighboring District Three whipped into the parking lot still doing forty miles per hour when he realized the lot was already full of police vehicles. He hit the first police unit which then slammed into two more. The young cop had an immediate flash of his testicles hanging from the flagpole at District Three station and he knew he was in deep trouble.

The suspect was taken to the ground by four officers and handcuffed, one retrieving the gun off the counter. The young clerk walked quietly around the counter and slapped Matt in the face as hard as she could screaming, "you told him to shoot me u son of a bitch!" The store, which was full of uniformed cops who were astonished and one asked Matt if he wanted her arrested as well. He told them to ignore what happened because he understood her frustration.

A supervisor had to be called to investigate the crash of the police cars. The Lieutenant told Matt that he should go on home and that they would take care of everything involving the robbery and that Matt should complete his statement the next day when he came to work. Matt was almost home when he realized that he had left the ice cream on the shelf at the store. Matt drove back to the store and picked it up but had a problem when the clerk refused to accept payment saying he had saved her life. Matt laid a five dollar bill on the counter and walked back to his car.

Matt's mother was watching the evening news when Matt walked into the apartment. The story said an unidentified police officer had foiled an armed robbery at the corner of Eighth and Linn Streets in the past hour and his mother got an odd look as Matt was carrying a bag with United Dairy Farmers stamped in bold print. Matt told her the story as they sat down for dinner. As they enjoyed the ice cream, Matt told his mother that the living arrangements were not working and asked if she wanted the apartment since she had made friends in the building and was working downtown. She said she wanted to continue to live there and Matt told her he would start looking for a new place.

***

Matt reported for work the next day intent on completing the paperwork from yesterday's incident. He was told by the desk officer to report to the Supervisors Office. The Sergeant behind the desk in the office told Matt that his training officer had taken a sick day and that Matt would be working alone for the shift. Matt was told that he would be handling reports and be a cover car and would not be working an assigned beat.

Matt walked into roll call and was immediately handed a run to Schomberg Elementary school to take a theft report. Matt sat through the briefing and then walked out to his cruiser to take the report. Matt got into the new Dodge Charger and a strange feeling began to overwhelm him. This would be the first time that he was alone in a police vehicle and was actually his own boss and that was scaring him a bit. He started the car and drove slowly toward the school trying to shake the fear and anticipation of riding alone.

Matt walked into the school office and was greeted by a receptionist who told him that $140 had been stolen from a desk drawer in an office. She took Matt to that office and Matt saw that the office door was open and no one was in the room. The desk drawer that contained the money in an envelope was also unlocked. Matt knew that the likelihood of finding the money or who took it was almost non-existent. The receptionist told Matt that the money was intended for a fourth grade field trip to a hockey game, but that was not going to happen due to the theft. Matt thanked the woman for her help and decided to return to the District to fill out the report. He was driving away from the school when he passed a bank with an outdoor ATM machine. He parked his cruiser and walked back to the ATM and withdrew $140 from his checking account. He put the cash into a bank envelope and shoved it into his shirt pocket. He got back into his car and drove to the District where he walked into the Supervisors office, handed the Sergeant the envelope and asked him to take it to the school. He told the Sergeant not to tell them where it came from. The Sergeant smiled and took the envelope from Matt.

The Sergeant delivered the envelope to the principal of the school and she asked him where it came from. He told her that it was from an anonymous source and left it there. It did not take an investigator to determine that it came from the officer that took the report and the principal picked up her phone and called Channel 12 News to give them the story. A videographer and a reporter showed up at the school and interviewed the fourth graders who now would be able to go to the hockey game. The kids called the police officer a hero and wanted to thank him in person. Upon completing their interviews, the reporter called the Public Information Officer at CPD for permission to interview the officer in front of District One police station. The P.I.O. said she would attempt to arrange it, but that it was up to the officer as to whether or not he wanted to be interviewed. Matt was in the line at the drive through waiting for his lunch when the call came for him to return to the District. He walked in the back entrance and was surprised when the first officer to see him began clapping. That drew the attention of other officers who also applauding as well. Matt was shocked when he saw the Police Chief in the back side of the room clapping as well.

The P.I.O. told Matt he was under no obligation to do the interview, but Matt agreed to it grudgingly. The P.I.O. introduced him to Debra Fixen, who told Matt that she was married to a retired cop and that she would do nothing to make him look bad on the air. The interview went very smoothly and Matt went back out on patrol.

The emergency tones dropped and the County notified all agencies of a pursuit southbound on I-75 toward the city. Moments later a Sergeant called communications to advise he had taken a position on the interstate to deploy Stop-Sticks, a plastic tube containing metal spikes which slowly deflate the tires of a vehicle. Matt decided to move toward the interstate when he heard screaming into the radio that an officer had been struck by a vehicle on I-75 near the Harrison Avenue exit. Matt drove down the exit ramp without even a thought that he would be traveling the wrong way on the Interstate during daylight hours. Matt drove north in the southbound lanes up the berm of the road startling drivers moving southbound. When he arrived at the crash, Matt saw the officer on the pavement and moved his police car across two lanes in order to shield the officer from being struck again.

The two Paramedics were just sitting down to lunch at the firehouse when the call came in that a police officer had been struck on I-75. They ran toward their rescue unit and started toward the crash when they were advised by radio to drive the wrong way north on southbound I-75 as the interstate had been shut down completely.

Matt checked the officer on the ground and could see bone protruding from his right leg. The sergeant's breathing was thready and weak and there was blood oozing out of his left ear. Matt saw the paramedic unit coming up the interstate and tried his best to comfort the officer. Immediately upon arriving the paramedics called for Air Care, the University of Cincinnati medical helicopter. It would be able to land on the interstate since it was shut down. Air Care had just completed a run and was still airborne, so it took less than three minutes until it touched down on I-75. On board were a trauma surgeon and two registered nurses and they found that the paramedics had already air splinted the leg, so the officer was ready for transport. They loaded the officer into the back of the helicopter and flew toward University Hospital, which is a Level One trauma center.

Matt went to the truck that hit the officer to see if anyone was injured. The man and his son were both fine and the driver told Matt that he had been driving southbound in the center lane when he looked into the rear mirror and saw all of the police vehicles involved in the chase. It appeared to him that the car being pursued was going to hit his truck and he veered to the left to get out of the way. The man said he did not see the officer until he hit him. Matt stood and talked with the driver until the Traffic Safety Unit arrived to complete the report. Matt was just glad that the sergeant was still alive.

Matt entered the rear entrance of the District and the tension and sadness was readily apparent. Matt overheard one officer saying that the Sergeant had been taken into surgery and was listed as extremely critical. Matt felt an overwhelming urge to cry, which he found strange since this was a man he had never met. He thought about the fact that he had not cried at the funeral of his own father and began to understand the bond that the badge they both wore had on him.

Matt walked to his car and called his mother to tell her he would not be home for dinner. He had decided to go to University Medical Center to offer his condolences to the family of the Sergeant. As he drove to the hospital, all he could think about was the fact that he only had one more day until his three days off and how much he needed those days to unwind from the stress he was feeling. Matt had been invited to join two other cops on the houseboat one of them owned.

Matt parked in front of the hospital and saw the line of television news trucks. Thinking he would be filmed walking into the hospital, Matt grabbed his white hat off the seat as he was getting out of his car. Matt was approaching the front entrance when he saw a female news anchor from the FOX affiliate moving quickly toward him with her cameraman right behind. The anchor shoved a microphone under his chin and asked for a comment on what he knew. Matt smiled meekly and said he did not have any information and walked toward the front door. The anchor gave him a look that could kill and stormed away. Matt walked up to the information desk and asked the woman where the surgical waiting room was located. She smiled at him and pointed toward a bank of elevators and told him to go to the fifth floor and turn left.

Matt got off the elevator and made the left hand turn down a hallway. He found the door marked "Surgical Waiting Area" and opened the door to see ten cops in uniform and a woman and two small children seated in chairs against the back wall. A cop walked up and told Matt that the woman and children were the Sergeant's and that the Police Chief had just left. Matt walked up to the woman, introduced himself, and told how he was the first officer to arrive at the scene of the crash. The woman thanked him for coming and went back to tending to the two children. Matt stayed for almost two hours making small talk with the other cops, none of which he had ever seen before. A doctor entered the waiting room and told the people that the Sergeant was in the recovery room and that the surgery had gone well. He told everyone the Sergeant was not out of the woods and that it would be touch and go for the next few days. When the doctor left the room, Matt decided that it was time for him to leave as well. Matt drove home feeling a little better knowing the cop was still alive and fighting.

***

Matt walked down the hall to the roll call room when Liza grabbed him by the arm. She told him that they were skipping the briefing because they had been detailed to provide uniform assistance to the Southern Ohio Fugitive Apprehension Task Force. SOFAST is operated by the US Marshal Service and focuses its attention on violent offenders who were wanted on drug and weapons offenses. They drove into the parking lot set up as a staging area at approximately the same time as three other marked police cars arrived.

Each was assigned to a team and Matt and Liza would be working with Team 4. Charlie Daws was the team supervisor, a burly man with a beard, who appeared to be in his early fifties. He had three other plainclothes people, one from Cincinnati Police, one from the Sheriff's Department and the fourth from the US Marshal's Office... The team was told they would be traveling to a residence on Back Street to serve a sealed indictment against a male named Argenta Wilson whose street name was "hot dog". The team members received a flyer with a picture of the suspect, which caused Liza to laugh and tell Matt that Wilson had a striking resemblance to a hot dog. The suspect was twenty-three years old, six feet three inches tall and weighed one hundred fifty pounds. Wilson had a history of being armed and of fighting with cops. The two uniformed cops were told they would take a position in an alley in the rear of the two story house and provide support if they were needed. The plainclothes officers were all wearing raid jackets with the word "POLICE" emblazoned on the front and the back.

Matt was driving and pulled into the alleyway close enough to see the rear of the house. He and Liza were sitting aimlessly in the police car when they heard the sound of the battering ram pulverizing the front door. Seconds later "hot dog" dove out of the second floor window, rolled up into a ball, and hit the ground. He got up immediately and started running through the back yards. Liza was out of the car in an instant totally surprising Matt and was hot on the trail of the runner.

The chase headed east over a couple of fences with Liza appearing to gain ground. Matt was a decent distance behind the two and was trying to broadcast the foot pursuit while trying to keep up. The suspect was leaping four-foot high fences like a high jumper and Liza was keeping pace with him even though she was weighed down with a gun belt and a bulletproof vest on. Matt was not having the same amount of success, having to vault the fences using one hand as a brace. Matt was able to keep both of them in sight, but the gap was widening.

Matt saw the suspect make a left turn when he reached the street and then lost sight of both him and his partner. When Matt reached the street he had totally lost sight of them and he was broadcasting his location for responding units when he heard the sound of a single gunshot. Matt saw a cement path up ahead on his left and ran full speed. The cement turned out to be an alley and he immediately saw his partner with her gun in her hand and the suspect on the pavement in the alley. He called in the officer involved shooting and asked for a rescue unit, and a supervisor.

Liza looked at Matt with wide eyes and asked if Matt had seen the suspect's gun. She said she had seen a gun in his waistband and that he appeared to reach for it once they entered the alley. Matt said he had lost sight of the two and that he never saw a weapon on the suspect. As sirens wailed to get to them, the two rolled Wilson over to find the gun, but it was not there. Matt said he would follow the trail backwards once things settled down and would find where Wilson had tossed the gun.

The scene was now total chaos. Cops and firemen flooded the scene and the crumpled body of Wilson was pronounced dead by the paramedics. Homicide detectives and a Lieutenant took Liza out to a marked police car and got her away from the scene just before the news trucks arrived. A Lieutenant approached Matt and asked if he saw the gun that Liza was claiming the suspect had. Matt told the boss that he was too far behind the foot pursuit to really see what the suspect had and that Seemoan was only a few feet behind the suspect throughout the chase.

Matt was ordered to drive down to the CIS unit and give a statement as soon as he could get back to his police car. Matt walked back trying to go the exact route as the foot pursuit in reverse in order to find the gun. He had no doubt that his partner had seen a gun but, unless it was located, she was in serious trouble. Matt checked the ground, in the trees and the bushes but could not find a weapon. He decided that he needed to make someone aware of the exact route that was traveled so that they could canvas that area and locate the weapon before someone else found it and removed it.

Matt walked into the CIS unit and was met by a couple of detectives who took him to an interview room to get his statement. He walked the two detectives step-by-step though the chase and what he saw when he turned into the alley. He told the two guys that he had no doubt that Liza saw a weapon on Wilson and that they needed to get out and find it. The two detectives told Matt to return to the alley and help with the search for the gun.

When Matt arrived to the place in the alley they had parked the Lieutenant from Homicide and the Captain of District One immediately met him. They told him to follow the path of the foot chase exactly as it had gone. The three walked together with eight more cops in a line behind them checking every blade of grass and every bush in hopes of finding the gun. The group had to climb over all the fences and re-form so they did not miss anything. They were unable to find anything when they reached the street. The three made the left turn toward the alley when Matt saw a house on the left with a gutter spout. The District One Captain called and requested a fire truck respond to meet them. When the fire truck arrived, the Captain told the firemen he needed a ladder to get up to see what was in the drain. Two detectives climbed onto the roof of the house and began searching, when they found a .22 caliber handgun lodged in the drain. The fingerprints on the gun would tell them if the gun belonged to the suspect, but it appeared to validate the claim of the officer that Wilson did have a gun. The gun was carefully bagged by the detectives and driven to the crime lab.

Matt quickly called Liza's cell phone, but she did not answer. He yelled into the phone that they had found the gun and wanted to be sure she was okay.

Matt returned to the District and finished out his daily report. He knew that he needed the next three days to be stress free as he felt he was losing his mind. A veteran District One cop had invited him to spend a couple of days on his houseboat in Indiana and Matt was looking forward to it.

CHAPTER EIGHTEEN

Matt woke up early and began packing a gym bag for the houseboat packing only what he thought he would need for the two days on the boat. He took his gun out of the holster and then thought better of taking it with him. He also was not going to take his cell phone because he did not want to be able to be reached.

The houseboat was moored on Brookville Lake in Indiana. Brookville is a small town about fifty miles west of Cincinnati and serves as a summer recreation area for people within a one hundred mile radius. The agreement was that Matt and the other cop invited would provide the food and drink and the owner of the boat would cover the boat's operation expenses. Matt got off of I-74 at the Brookville exit and stopped at a liquor store where he bought a case of beer for the boat. A few miles later he found a grocery store and bought steaks, hamburgers, ice and chips. He also bought lunchmeat, bacon, eggs and bread so they would be set.

He arrived in the parking lot and saw Dave Thomas, a twenty-two year veteran of Cincinnati Police, and a guy he did not know waiting for him. The third member of the crew was a Hamilton County deputy named Dale Henwert. Henwert, told Matt that his nickname was Hondo, was a twenty year veteran of the Sheriff's Department. Matt would later find out that Henwert was a non-drinker and a nonsmoker who married his childhood sweetheart and had five children. They loaded all the food and drinks onto the boat and started out onto the pristine lake just after eleven o'clock for a few days of fun and relaxation.

Matt really did not know Thomas well and was surprised when the offer to join him was made. He knew a bank robbery suspect had shot Thomas in the right shoulder a few years earlier. The robber was then shot and killed by Thomas in a shootout with police. He also had heard that Thomas had become addicted to painkillers and was a hard drinker.

The day reminded Matt of his days in California. The sun was beating down on them and the skies were a bright blue, but there was a gentle breeze that was keeping him cool and relaxed. The boat was a couple of miles from their mooring point when Thomas turned off the engine and let the boat just float. Henwert pointed toward the side of the boat where the fishing reels and bait were kept in two long wood storage bins. Matt had never been fishing and did not know how to attach the bait to the hook or how to throw the line into the water. As Matt sat in his chair on the deck of the boat he felt an inner peace that he had never before experienced. The only sounds he heard were those of a radio softly playing oldies and the occasional roar of a speedboat pulling a skier. Thomas told him that the air personality on the oldies station had retired from the Police Department as a Lieutenant.

It was getting late in the afternoon and Matt was feeling the effects of the sun beating down upon him. He climbed down the ladder of the boat and immersed himself into the cooling waters of the lake. He watched with amazement as Hondo did a cannonball off the side of the boat splashing water all over the now inebriated Thomas, who scowled and launched an empty beer can at him, missing by at least twenty feet. Hondo had to swim out to retrieve the can which was floating on top of the lake. Matt climbed back onto the boat and reached into his bag to get a tee shirt in the hope of not looking like a cooked lobster the next day. He also rummaged in the bag until he found his ball cap that displayed the logo of his favorite baseball team, the LA Dodgers. He placed the cap on his head which drew another scowl from the drunken cop and another beer can that missed its target and landed in the lake. They had to use a net to retrieve the second empty can so it would not float down the lake.

Matt had just sat back down in the chair when the fishing reel bowed forward. Matt grabbed the reel, and with the help of Hondo, rocked back and forth trying to reel in a fish that definitely did not want to be dinner for humans. Hondo grabbed the net and when they finally got the fish into the boat, it proved to be a five pound trout. Hondo got a picture of Matt holding the fish while Thomas went into the galley. He returned with a cutting board, a cleaver and a filet knife. Thomas whacked the head off the fish and tossed it into the lake, telling the other cops that it would be dinner for the fish. He expertly sliced the trout from the fins to the tail and then turned it over and got two perfect filets. He then tossed the skeletal remains into the lake. Thomas dropped the filets into the ice chest and it was decided that it was time to move on. Hondo started the engine of the houseboat and proceeded further away from the dock until he found an alcove off the lake that had no boats. He dropped the anchor and the three pulled out the grill to cook the fish Matt had caught. When they were done eating, the three cleaned the grill and loaded a trash bag with the empty beer cans to be dumped the next day.

It was now totally dark in the alcove and they had to find a flashlight to get into the galley to turn on the lights of the houseboat. Matt and Thomas were sitting in chairs drinking their beer when they heard the sounds of a boat motor getting louder as it got closer. Matt intently watched the black entrance to the cove for whatever was approaching when a set of floodlights lit up the houseboat. The floodlights also illuminated the red and blue light bar on the top of the approaching boat. The Indiana Conservation boat eased up along side of their boat and Matt gingerly reached into the bag at his side, picking up a leather case with his forefinger and thumb so as not to get shot by cops thinking he was reaching for a gun.

The two conservation cops were about the same age as Matt and the passenger, in as gruff a voice as he could muster, demanded to know what they were doing there. Matt slowing opened the leather case showing his badge and identification card which was immediately snatched away from him by the conservation officer. As the cop looked at the badge and ID, Matt told them that they were all cops and had just looked for a place to relax and spend the night. The driver of the conservation boat wanted to know who had driven the boat since it was clear that Matt and Thomas were inebriated. Hondo came out from around the corner and told the two cops that he was a non-drinker and he was the driver. The conservation cops laughed and told them to have a great night. They announced that they would not be returning again tonight and to enjoy their time on the lake. The two cops turned their boat away and slowly pulled out of the cove and out of sight.

About a half hour passed with dead silence when Matt heard the sound of another engine. He commented that the conservation cops had told them they would not be returning and he was confused. A boat pulled up along side and Matt could see three women, who appeared to be in their late forties or early fifties dressed in swimsuits. As the boats touched the one closed to the houseboat announced that the women were out looking for a party and saw the lights of the houseboat. Matt invited them onto the houseboat and then stretched out his arm to help them. Matt marveled at the muscle tone of the three women in their one-piece suits. The spokesperson introduced herself as Katelyn and the other two as Danice and Danielle. While Matt was busy helping the ladies onto the houseboat, Hondo tied off their boat. Thomas disappeared into the galley and returned with two large beach towels which he tossed onto the shore and motioned the women to join him on the shore. Matt got stuck with lugging the ice chest off the boat. Hondo announced that this was not something for him to participate in and went into the galley to go to sleep.

The five on the shore were enjoying their beers when Katelyn stood up and announced she wanted to swim, but that she did not want to get her suit wet. In a split second the suit hit the ground and she was standing naked in front of them. As if on cue, the other two women stood up and disrobed and the three jumped into the lake. They demanded the men take off their swimwear and join them. The five frolicked in the water for a short period with everyone being groped and splashed like a group of children at play.

They all climbed back onto the shore and Matt went onto the deck of the houseboat to get towels for everyone to dry off. They sat naked on the shore and Danielle expressed concern about being busted by boat cops if they did not get clothes on. Matt laughed and told the women that they were all cops and that the boat cops had already been and gone. Since there were now three women and only two men, Katelyn and Denice snuggled up with Matt while Danielle laid next to Thomas. Katelyn and Denice kissed on Matt and each other and they all played until they tired out. The five slept on the shore until the sunlight woke them in the morning.

Hondo was on the deck and invited the ladies to join them for breakfast, but the ladies politely declined and got back onto their boat. As they left the ladies thanked the men for a great time and then roared off to their next adventure.

After breakfast the men took the houseboat back to the dock to dump garbage and send Matt out for more liquid refreshment. When Matt returned Thomas guided the houseboat in the opposite direction of where they had been for another day of fishing. The three men sat on the deck and Matt listened as the two older cops exchanged stories. Thomas told a tale of receiving a radio dispatch of a man being hit by a train at four o'clock in the morning. When he arrived, they had already found the torso of the victim, but he had no head. Ten cops wandered both sides of the tracks until one came up from a valley holding the man's head in his left hand announcing, "Anyone looking for this?"

Hondo told a story of chasing a robbery suspect through the rear yards of an orphanage late at night when the man reached his hand into his pants just as he was transmitting his location into the radio.

Cops from all over Hamilton County heard him clearly say, "FREEZE or I will blow your fucking head off!" After the event was over, Hondo was told to meet a Sergeant in the parking lot of a restaurant. Hondo pulled his cruiser next to the Sergeant who instructed him to extend his arm out the window. The Sergeant slapped the back of Hondo's hand and advised him never to do that again. The three cops just sat and laughed and enjoyed the lake until it was time for dinner. Hondo drove the boat and found another cove that they could make their own for the night and they grilled steaks and called it a night shortly after darkness. Matt slept in the chair on the deck while the other two used the beds below. Matt was the first to wake and fixed breakfast for them after which they went back to the dock to clean and secure the boat in its slip. Matt thanked Thomas profusely for inviting him and went to his car to drive home.

CHAPTER NINETEEN

Matt drove slowly through Brookville on his way to the Interstate because he was in no real hurry to get home. As he drove, he reflected on the peacefulness and serenity of the last two days and was now seriously considering the purchase of a houseboat of his own which he would actually live on. On his three days off each week he would be able to take the boat out and be at peace with the water. He knew there were docks along the Ohio River close enough for him to get to work and his mother would have the apartment to herself.

Matt had just opened the door of the apartment when his mother demanded to know where his cell phone was. Matt meekly pointed toward an end table next to the couch where it had sat for the last two days. His mother told him that Liza had called several times as had the Captain of District One. There were also a couple of calls from a Sergeant whose name she could not remember.

Matt picked up the cell phone and turned it on, immediately seeing that he had eighteen missed calls. He checked his voicemail to find the first call from Liza who said it was important that he call her immediately. The second was from the Captain who said to call him immediately upon receiving the message. The next was from a

Sergeant Bailey who identified himself as being with the Internal Investigation Section of the police department.

Matt called Liza and got her voicemail. He left her a quick message that he had been out of town and to return his call. He then called the Captain who told him he needed to immediately contact IIS because they wanted to talk to him. He hung up with the Captain and called the number left by Sergeant Bailey who told him to report to an address on West Eighth Street at nine am the next morning in civilian clothes and that would constitute his work day. Matt asked the Sergeant what it was about, but was told that this was an order and that he would find out when he arrived.

The quizzical look on Matt's face when he hung up the phone caused his mother to ask what was wrong. Matt tried to explain he had been ordered to a meeting, but his mother had no clue what Internal Investigations meant. He explained that the unit was made up of cops who investigate possible misconduct by other cops. Cops are not generally well liked by the public and the cops assigned to Internal had the double whammy of not being liked by other cops. The members of the unit were known as the "rat squad" and "headhunters," but it was also known to be the fast track to promotions and most of the executives of the police department spent some of their career in the unit.

Matt told his mother that he was going for a run and that he would take her out to dinner and tell her about the lake. He left the apartment and walked down to the riverfront to run east along the river. During the run he tried to sort out what the headhunters could possibly want to talk to him about, then remembered they were investigating the incident with Liza and that could well be why she needed to talk to him so urgently.

Matt took his mom to a Wong's Chinese restaurant in the downtown area and told her most of what happened on the boat. He left out the parts he didn't think she would want to know about. He told her about his thoughts to live on a houseboat and received a less than enthusiastic response.

Matt went to bed early and was putting on a suit and tie for the morning meeting. He began to feel like he was going to a job interview and getting very nervous about what was to come. He still had not heard back from Liza and tried, without success, to call her while driving to the location. He pulled into the parking lot on Eighth Street at the address he had been given to find that it was multiple office buildings. He was glad that each building had its own address in big print on the front entrance. He walked into the lobby and immediately saw a security guard seated at a desk.

The guard looked up from the magazine he was reading and knew instantly that the guy in the lobby was a cop. Going back to his magazine, he told Matt to turn left when he got off the elevator. Matt walked up to the door of Suite 310 and noticed that there was no sign on the door that would indicate what was inside. He opened the door to see a waiting area with a receptionist behind a glass partition. The woman at the desk sternly asked him his last name and told him to have a seat and he would be escorted back.

Matt sat in one of the chairs in the waiting room that was devoid of any pictures or magazines or a television. There was nothing in the room other than four chairs and the room was totally silent. He sat in the chair for what seemed like an eternity, but was really only about twenty minutes when a man in a suit opened the door to the inner office and called him in.

Nothing was said as the man led Matt back toward the rear of the office. Approximately halfway back, a man who appeared to be in his late forties, got up from his desk and followed both men to a room that looked like an interview room in a police station. Matt saw a table and three chairs. One chair was on one side of the table, the other two on the other side. The man who called Matt in pointed to the lone chair for him to sit and the other two sat on the other side. The second man had a legal pad and a pen. The first man introduced himself as Sergeant Don Bailey of the Internal Investigation Section and told Matt that the interview would be both audio and video taped. He told Matt that the interview would begin with Garrity warnings and read from a sheet of paper.

The warnings are named after a United States Supreme Court case which authorized employers to require public employees to truthfully answer any and all questions asked and that failure to answer or tell the truth would result in termination of employment from the Police Department for insubordination. Matt was told that he had a right to have a union representative or an attorney present at the interview, but that they would not be allowed to speak.

When Matt acknowledged that he understood the warning, the investigator told him to walk them through the events leading up to the shooting by Officer Seemoan. Matt, slowly and meticulously, took them through the morning from the time at the briefing room through to the walk-through with the Captain.

The second investigator, who had not spoken a word up to this point, laid his pen on the pad and looked directly into Matt's eyes with a steely glare. He told Matt that he only had one question and that was he wanted to know when Matt threw the gun that was recovered up into the gutter.

The shocked and stunned look on Matt's face said it all. Matt slid his chair back away from the table and told the two cops that the interview was now over and that he wanted an attorney present if they were going to make moronic allegations. Bailey ordered Matt to sit back down and pulled a cell phone out of his pocket. Bailey dialed a number and handed Matt the phone. A voice on the other end answered "FOP LODGE 60, how can I help you?" Matt told the secretary he was at Internal and needed an attorney as there were allegations that he had committed a criminal act. The secretary immediately connected Matt to the FOP president, who said that the union attorney would be there in less than half an hour. Bailey asked Matt if he wanted lunch brought in because he was on City time and was not free to leave. The two investigators left and returned with a ham and cheese sandwich and a can of iced tea for Matt while they waited for the attorney to arrive.

When the attorney got there, he told the investigators to shut off all recording devices and to leave the interview room. Matt told the attorney the allegation made and made it clear he had no idea where they got that idea. The attorney explained that the invocation of Garrity made him immune from criminal prosecution, but did not protect his job.

With the attorney standing behind him, Matt emphatically told the investigators that he did not throw anything into a gutter or anywhere else. The older cop asked how he knew the gun was there and Matt explained that the only time the suspect was out of his sight was when he turned left onto the street and Matt was looking upward during the walk-through and saw the gutter. He reminded the headhunters that it was the Captain who called for a ladder from the fire truck and that it was Homicide detectives who actually recovered the gun.

Matt was told he was free to leave and that he was to return to his regular assignment the following day. As Matt got ready to walk out of the room the old cop said he had one more question for him. Matt stopped and turned around with his lawyer and the old cop told Matt there was a problem they were unable to solve. The gun that was recovered had been wiped clean of fingerprints and the prints on the bullet casings were too smudged to identify. The old cop asked Matt if it was possible that Officer Seemoan had tossed the gun into the gutter. Matt took his time formulating an answer, then told the headhunters there were two problems with that scenario. The first was that if Liza was going to plant a gun, she would have placed it where it would be likely to be found. The second problem in their theory was that she would have had to have tossed the gun prior to shooting the suspect because Matt was in the alley within ten seconds of the shot being fired and Liza was never more than two feet from him until she was transported to the Homicide Unit. Matt left the interview room without even a thank you for his cooperation, which he found extremely disheartening because, after all, they were all cops.

Matt was visibly shaken as he left the office with the lawyer. Matt drove home trying to sort out the day's events and decided that Liza may have been ordered not to talk to him.

CHAPTER TWENTY

Matt parked in the employee lot and prepared for his shift. He walked in through the Police entrance and was told that he was to report to the supervisor's office by a cop standing by the briefing room. Matt walked into the Sergeants Office and was handed a letter on City letterhead. The letter said that Matt's probation period had ended and that he would be reassigned to District Three beginning the following Sunday on the four o'clock pm until two o'clock am shift. Matt was now a full fledged Cincinnati Police Officer. The Sergeant told Matt that his off days had changed and he would be off two days until his new assignment took effect.

Matt soared through the shift as if he was walking on a cloud. All of his hard work and effort had come to fruition. He was now officially on his own as a police officer.

The City of Cincinnati is divided into five geographical police districts. There were seven until the early 1970s when District One and District Two, that both shared the downtown district, were combined. District Four and District Seven, both of which were in dilapidated buildings, were merged into a centrally located new facilty. District Three covers the western side of Cincinnati from the western edge of downtown along the river to the county line and north from the river to the western City limits. It also presents some challenges in that the City limits are intertwined though Delhi and Green Townships, both of which are their own jurisdictions. Hamilton County, Ohio has thirty-two separate police jurisdictions, almost as many as the State of Rhode Island.

Matt went out on his day off and purchased a street map from a local convenience store. He wanted to learn the major thoroughfares in District Three because he knew that he would be getting lost while he was working. Matt drove out River Road looking at the industries on the Ohio River and the lower class residences on the north side of the road. He reached a sign that said leaving the City of Cincinnati, but continued west because he was enjoying the scenery. About three miles later, he was shocked to see a sign welcoming people to Saylor Park inside the City of Cincinnati limits.

Matt continued his ride until he reached the Village of Addyston, Ohio, a town which only has 2,000 residents, Matt saw that there was a large dock for boats, reminding him of buying a houseboat and this seemed like a great place to house it. He drove back along Road until he was back in Delhi Township when he decided to tour it as well. He turned onto Anderson Ferry Road, a road named after the Anderson Ferry which transports motor vehicles across the river from Ohio into Kentucky. As he was driving up the road, he saw signs inviting people to the Delhi Skirt game which he found to be very intriguing. Matt saw a Township cop parked in a lot and stopped to ask the officer what in the hell the skirt game is. The cop laughed and told him it was a combination of celebrities, politicians and members of the Delhi Athletic Association who dressed in drag and played a softball game for charity. Matt thought this would be something he could take his mother to watch because it sounded like a fun time. He got lost a few times trying to find his way back to downtown, but found the major roadways to navigate around the west side.

Matt told his mother that he was taking her to a softball game that sounded like fun. She gave him a strange look, but dressed up for the evening. When they arrived at Delhi Park she laughed as she saw men with beards wearing skirts and dresses.

The event was more farcical slapstick than a softball game, but watching his mother laugh was much more important than the event itself. Matt knew that his mother needed something outside of living in an apartment to really become alive again.

***

Matt had to park on a side street because the parking lot at District Three was so small. District Three is the oldest police facility in Cincinnati and is scheduled for replacement in 2014. It is a two story brick building that is almost seventy years old. Matt had to enter through the public entrance because he was not provided the code to enter through the employee door.

Matt approached the desk officer who was about the same age as Matt. The young cop appeared to be really unhappy being stuck on a desk and was there as a punishment. Matt told the cop that he was there for his first day and the cop stuck out his arm and pointed toward a door. As Matt approached the door, the officer pushed the button buzzing the door open. Matt walked down a hallway until he found the Supervisors Office and walked up to the Sergeant sitting at a desk. He handed the Sergeant his transfer papers. The Sergeant introduced himself as Will Grace and got up from his seat to shake Matt's hand. Matt took notice that this man had a powerful grip.

The Sergeant walked out of the office and motioned Matt to follow him. Sgt. Grace told Matt that the Captain met with every new officer individually before they started their first shift. Captain Russ Newhall had a citywide reputation as an aggressive leader who would really rather still be a street cop. It was rumored in the other Districts that he handled radio calls when officers were tied up. Captain Newhall extended his hand out to Matt and welcomed him to the District Three family. Captain Newhall told Matt that he had high expectations of his cops and that loyalty to the citizens of Cincinnati was his top priority. He went on to say that anything less than a one hundred percent work ethic would not be tolerated.

Sergeant Grace took Matt to the basement where the locker rooms were located. The locker area had to be split into two sections to accommodate female officers, but there was a single bathroom and shower which had two entrance doors each with a lock. Matt had brought a duffle bag containing a spare uniform that his mother had packed and neatly folded for him. The two then went up to the second floor where the District detectives were packed in like sardines. They went back down the main floor and the Sergeant took Matt to the roll call room for his first shift briefing, wishing him success at District Three.

Matt walked into the room where the cops were milling around waiting for the briefing to begin. Matt only saw two cops that were in his Academy class. Dave Plotts was a guy who did not want to be friends with anyone in the class and Dawn Taylor, who had been part of his study group. Dawn saw Matt and waved from the other side of the room.

Matt sat at the table and quietly waited until the Sergeant came in to conduct the briefing. The Sergeant introduced Matt to the shift and told him that he would be running beat 3201 which covers the river area of the District. Matt was told that the cruiser was equipped with a radar unit which meant that Matt was expected to write two traffic tickets in his shift. Some call that a quota, but Matt remembered what he had been told by Liza that an officer should witness at least one traffic violation for each shift that they work.

Matt went into the parking lot and found his Dodge Charger cruiser. He placed his bag on the passenger seat containing his street map, a second pair of handcuffs, and his white hat.

Matt walked around the cruiser checking for damage because he would be held accountable for any damage he did not report. He tested the overhead lights and siren to assure they were operating properly, then started the car and left the parking lot. Matt turned right out of the driveway and pulled up to a red light on Warsaw Avenue. As he was sitting there, a yellow Ford Mustang blew the red light almost getting hit broadside by a car. Matt smiled because he was going to get the first of the two tickets quickly. He fell in behind the Mustang and activated the overhead lights, but the Mustang did not pull over. Matt blew the siren to get the male driver's attention, but that did not work either. Matt saw that the driver was a young white male, so he assumed the kid had his music blaring so he wound the siren and used the air horn to get the driver's attention.

When the Mustang stopped, Matt had to grin as he entered the personalized license plate SMOKE*EM into the police computer to check for warrants. When the car came back clean, Matt walked up to the driver who already had his license, registration and insurance card hanging out of the window. Matt asked the young male driver why he ran the light and the kid said that he was late for work and had been told that he would be fired if he was late again. Matt walked back to his cruiser thinking that he would cut the guy a break until he ran the driver's record and found that he had been issued a speeding ticket just two days earlier.

Matt wrote out the ticket for disregarding the traffic control device and walked back to the Mustang to have the driver sign the citation. He handed the driver his copy and returned to his cruiser.

Matt was entering the citation onto his daily activity report when he received a radio run to a neighbor dispute. Matt had been on this street during his tour of District Three so he knew the area was low income dilapidated houses. He pulled up in front of the house and walked to the front door where a black woman in a tattered blue dress was awaiting him. The woman told Matt that her neighbor's nine year old son had come to her side yard, dropped his pants and peed on her tomato plants. Matt walked the fifty feet between the houses and knocked on the door. He knocked a second and then a third time when a large white woman wearing a Bengals football jersey finally answered the door. Matt told the woman that he needed to talk to her son and she told him she had five sons. Matt asked her if one of them was nine years old and the woman, with a defiant scowl on her face, told Matt that she had ordered her son to go over and piss on her neighbor's plants in retaliation for her neighbor bringing her dog into her garden to pee and shit.

Matt told the woman he could arrest both of them and that, if he had to return for another complaint, they would both be going to jail. Matt returned to the complainant's house and asked the woman if she had taken her dog into her neighbor's yard. The woman said that the dog chose where he wanted to do his "business." Matt told this lady that he did not like his time wasted and that if he had to come back for any reason, everyone was going to get arrested and a Judge could decide who did what to who!

Just as Matt advised communications that he was available, the dispatcher advised of an auto accident with persons trapped in the forty-four hundred block of River Road. The dispatcher stated that a tanker truck had jackknifed on top of a passenger car. Matt jumped into his cruiser and activated the lights and siren and arrived less than three minutes later. He could see a squashed car underneath the tanker as he approached. When he ran toward the car, he could see a young woman who was obviously dead in the driver's seat. He started to move to check on the driver when he heard a soft moaning sound coming from the rear seat area of the car. Matt laid flat on the pavement and looked into the rear window seeing a young boy and hearing moaning. Using his metal baton, Matt tried to clean the window of jagged glass so he could crawl in and extricate the boy from the car. Passerbys had run up asking how they could help. Matt told them to grab his legs and slowly pull him backward once he was able to secure the boy. As he climbed in through the window, Matt could hear the jagged glass shreading his police shirt, but his bulletproof vest was keeping the glass away from his body. Matt grabbed the boy and yelled to be pulled out, making sure the boy was protected from the glass chards sticking up from the window frame.

The child had just been pulled out when the first fire truck and a paramedic unit arrived at the scene. The paramedics placed the child on a stretcher and called for a medical helicopter to come and transport the child. The fire personnel located the driver of the truck who only had minor injuries and determined that the female driver of the car was, in fact, dead.

Matt smelled like he had rolled in diesel fuel and his shirt was destroyed. Because it was a fatality, he would not have to investigate the crash, as that was the responsibility of the traffic safety unit of the police department. Once those officers arrived, Matt drove back to the District glad that he had brought a second uniform that day.

Matt went into the locker area and stripped off his clothes to get a shower since there was diesel fuel in his hair as well. He was just coming out of the shower when the door to the ladies locker room, that he had forgotten to lock, opened and he saw Dawn looking at his naked body. Matt sheepishly grabbed a towel and wrapped himself, apologizing to Dawn for forgetting to lock the door. Matt could see a wry smile on the female cop's face as he scurried back into the men's area, hearing the click of the door lock being activated behind him.

Matt put the tattered clothing in a bag and took them up to the supervisor's office to requisition a new uniform, then returned to his cruiser. He had not quite reached the car when the emergency tones dropped and two cars were dispatched to a silent robbery alarm at a pharmacy on his beat. Matt called into communications and told them to cancel one of the units, as he was available to respond. The call was at the far end of River Road, almost ten miles from the District. Matt turned on the lights and siren and screamed out of the parking lot down to River Road, where he ran into the remnants of the rush hour traffic trying to get home. Matt had to navigate around the heavy traffic that had nowhere to go to get out of his way.

When Matt pulled up in front of the pharmacy, he was surprised to see four marked police cars already there. One said ADDYSTON POLICE, one was the Police Chief of CLEVES and the other two said DELHI POLICE on the doors. The owner of the pharmacy, who was standing outside talking to the cops, scoffed and said, "Glad you could finally make it!" Matt got on his radio and advised of the false alarm and cancelled the additional cars responding. He thanked the cops for covering the call, and decided to find somewhere to grab his dinner.

After eating, Matt went to find a spot to get his second ticket. He found a curved road that was desolate and looked like a track for a speedway. Bender Road comes out of Delhi so Matt had to make sure that he was actually within the City limits before he found a place to set up the radar unit. There was not a car that passed in either direction for almost twenty minutes and the first car was ten miles under the posted limit of thirty-five. It took another fifteen minutes until a Humvee rounded a curve and the radar locked in at sixty-three miles per hour. Matt wrote the citation and did not receive another call the rest of the shift.

***

Matt's second shift in the District started with a radio run for a car blocking a driveway in another beat. Matt had difficulty locating the street that the run was to, having to refer to his street guide several times. It took him almost twenty minutes to finally pull up at the address and the owner of the house came outside to tell him the car had just left. Matt waved at the owner and then drove to the end of the street to park and look at his street map.

The best route back to his beat was using South Road which was in Green Township. Matt was driving along when he caught up to a Ford Explorer that was having difficulty staying inside his own lane. Matt watched the Explorer drift left of center a number of times, but knew that Ohio law prohibited him from making a traffic stop for an offense that occurred outside of his jurisdiction. Matt called in on the radio and advised he was following a possible DUI on South Road and needed a County unit to make a traffic stop.

The Explorer ran a stop sign and made a sudden right hand turn onto a road with no street sign. Matt followed behind as the dispatcher advised both Green and Delhi Township cars were in route. The dispatcher asked for his current location and Matt was embarrassed to announce he had no clue where he was. The two vehicles crossed an intersection that told Matt they were on Devils Backbone Road and Matt told the dispatcher immediately. The Explorer made a sudden left turn and almost immediately crashed into a parked car.

Matt activated the overhead lights on the cruiser and ran up to make sure the driver was okay. The driver, who appeared to be in his early fifties, stammered some words Matt could not understand just as a Hamilton County cruiser arrived. It was followed by two Green Township cars and a Delhi Township cruiser. The deputy immediately advised the driver he was under arrest for Operating a Motor Vehicle While Under the Influence (OMVI) and took Matt's name and badge number as a witness. Matt sheepishly asked the Green Township cop to help him find South Road to get back to his beat. He told the cop that he was new to District Three and was lost. The Township cop led Matt all the way back to River Road and waved as he drove off.

Matt found a place on River Road to set up the radar unit and it took only minutes until he had his first speeder. The problem was that it was another Cincinnati cop. Matt returned to his spot and made the second stop which turned out to be an off-duty deputy sheriff. People often complain that cops get preferential treatment in traffic stops and they are right. Cops know that other cops, inside or outside of their jurisdiction, will always stop and offer aid to another cop in trouble, where the public will likely keep on driving. The third stop Matt made was a juvenile who was driving thirty miles over the posted speed limit. Matt cited the young man to Juvenile Court and then went for his dinner.

Matt spent the rest of the shift trying to get the second required ticket, but no one was biting. He tried sitting near a four way stop in the hope that someone would run a stop sign, but the cars either saw him or were just actually following the law. Matt decided to give up and just learn the roads in the area.

Matt showed up for roll call for his third day and was assigned beat 3209 which covers the northern part of the District and Interstate 74. This cruiser also was equipped with a radar unit as well and Matt headed toward I-74 immediately after roll call. Matt intended to go to a turnaround in the median, but saw a county cruiser already there clocking cars coming into the City from the County. Matt parked next to the county cop so he could clock cars leaving the City limits. The two cops chatted until the deputy clocked a Camaro at eighty-six miles per hour in the fifty-five mile per hour zone. The deputy waved to Matt as he drove off to chase the car.

Matt also did not have to wait long. He clocked a Toyota Camry at seventy-six miles per hour and took off to give chase. Matt could see that there were two females in the car which pulled over immediately when Matt turned on the overheads. Matt walked up to the car and was shocked to see that both of the young women were butt naked. The driver explained that the two were strippers driving to Indianapolis, Indiana for a new job and decided to have some fun with the truckers along the way. Matt mulled over the thought of writing a ticket, but decided it was not going to be worthwhile to have to testify that they were naked. He warned them that other cops might not be as forgiving and walked back to his cruiser.

The emergency tones sounded and broadcast that a Green Township officer had been fired upon at a bank robbery on North Bend Road. Matt knew, from driving to the lake, that North Bend Road was the next exit on I-74 and jumped on the radio announcing that he was responding. Matt turned on the siren and floored the gas pedal, driving like a madman west on the Interstate. He actually had to stop at the end of the exit ramp to allow a Hamilton County and a Cheviot Police cruiser to pass. Matt fell in behind the other two and they pulled into the bank lot together. The Township cop told the three cops that he pulled into the bank lot just as the robber came out of the front door. The robber fired four shots that hit the windshield of the cruiser. When the Township cop was able to roll out of the driver's seat, the suspect was gone.

There were now six cops and the Township officer who had been fired on. They broke into three two-man teams with Matt being hooked with the Cheviot cop. The Cheviot cop told Matt that he needed to go back to his cruiser and get something. The cop opened the trunk and pulled out the AR-15 assault rifle and the two went off on the search. They walked to the rear of an office building when Matt saw a line of garbage cans. The area around all but one of the cans was clean, but the last garbage can looked like it had been dumped. Matt signaled to the Cheviot cop, who walked over and kicked the can with all of his might. The lid of the can flew off and the suburban cop stuck the barrel of the rifle into the man's right ear telling him to come out of the can. The man whispered that he was stuck in the can that caused the two cops to break out in laughter. The Cheviot cop used his portable radio to call for a fire truck to respond which brought all of the cops in the area to this bizarre sight.

The fire truck pulled up and brought out the Jaws of Life to cut open the galvanized aluminum can. They had to move slowly and carefully because there was almost no space. It took the fire department almost forty-five minutes to extricate the man who was immediately handcuffed. The odor of the stay in the trash can was almost overwhelming and Matt was glad that he would not be the one to have to transport the suspect to jail.

Matt walked back to his cruiser and returned to his beat. He liked the fact he could take credit for a felony arrest on his activity log and not have to appear in court.

Matt decided to drive in North Bend Road to continue to learn the area. He got to the end of the road which stops at Harrison Avenue. Matt knew that Harrison was one of the major thoroughfares transecting the District, so he was happy with his decision. Matt saw a sign saying Habig's Restaurant and Home Cooking on it, so he decided to stop for a meal. Matt just hoped that he would actually get to sit and eat the meal without having to leave in the middle for a radio run. He was really in the mood for a home style meal. Matt sat at a table next to a family of four. The youngest of the children was glued on Matt's gun on his side. Matt smiled and waved at the youngster and got a big smile from the five or six year old in return. Matt sat and ate his meatloaf, mashed potatoes and corn undisturbed, but was shocked when he walked up to the cash register and was told the meal was free. He walked back to the table and laid a five dollar bill down as a tip for the server.

Matt cruised Harrison Avenue dropping off onto side streets to see if he could find his way back. Darkness was just setting in when he received a call to Nottingham Drive for a person shot. Nottingham Drive is the home of the Fay Apartments which is owned and operated by the Federal Housing and Urban Development. It consists of two streets with over one hundred units but has only one entrance and one exit. At one time the complex had its own police department under Federal authority. Matt turned off Baltimore Avenue into the complex and continued down Nottingham until his headlights shined on a body in the middle of the street. Matt blocked off the street with his cruiser and ran to the body and he immediately determined that the fortyish male black was dead.

Matt called for Homicide to respond and went to the trunk of the car to crime scene tape off the area. He wrapped the bright yellow tape around a telephone pole, then across the street to a street sign, then down the street to an electric pole. He was glad this cruiser had a full roll of tape as he took it back across the street and back to the original pole.

There had been a group of people standing around when Matt pulled up, and the numbers kept on growing. Once the tape was up, Matt began walking up to people asking if they had seen anything that would help in the investigation. It almost seemed that everyone he asked had the same script because all said they "didn't see nothing."

He finally located a woman who told him the victim's name and showed Matt where the victim lived. Matt and two detectives went to the house and found the door standing open. The three drew their guns and searched the small apartment finding blood on the carpet, but no one there. The detectives told Matt to secure the apartment while they went to find crime scene technicians to process this second location. Matt was standing at the door when a Lieutenant walked up and wanted to go inside. Matt smiled and told the Lt. that he would need to get the boss' name and badge number to put on the log so the Lieutenant could be subpoenaed for court. The Lt. walked away in a huff without ever entering the scene. Matt had to guard the apartment for about twenty minutes until the CSI's could get there.

The detectives told Matt that the man had died from two gunshot wounds to the chest, probably fired from a small caliber handgun. One of the older uniform cops told the detectives that the victim was known as a member of a gang called the Tot Lot Posse, which had been fragmented a few years earlier in a Cincinnati Police and FBI joint investigation. Matt spent the rest of the shift sitting in his cruiser blocking the street while the investigation progressed. Another shift had passed without the required number of traffic citations, but Matt hoped the bosses took into consideration his activity log. He did not want to get yelled at this early in his new District.

CHAPTER TWENTY-ONE

Matt had put in for two vacation days on the back side of his three days off to take his mother on a vacation. He felt she needed to get out of the apartment so he was taking her to Louisville, Kentucky and from there to Nashville, Tennessee. They decided to avoid the Interstate and use the back roads to make the trip more scenic. They were able to see the farmlands of Kentucky and pass through small towns where it appeared that time had stopped. Matt checked them into a pricey hotel in Louisville where their patio overlooked the Ohio River.

They enjoyed southern comfort food for dinner and took a tour of the downtown district in a horse drawn carriage. The next morning they had a southern traditional breakfast of grits, eggs and country ham and then drove to Churchill Downs, home of the Kentucky Derby. Their next stop was at a horse farm where Matt's mom rode a horse for the very first time. That evening they crossed over the Ohio River into Indiana and went to a casino where she won five hundred dollars playing the quarter slots. She screamed and jumped for joy and the people around her thought she had won the million dollar jackpot. Matt was seeing a trend that she was getting back into living and it made him feel really good.

They left Louisville and drove into Nashville where they checked into the hotel at the Grand Ol Opry. They walked the downtown area and attended a country western show that evening. The second day in Nashville was spent scooping out the architecture that made Nashville famous. They enjoyed a meal and called it an early night to make the five hour drive back to Cincinnati.

When Matt arrived at the District for roll call, he felt relaxed and ready for whatever was to come on his shift. He was given a station run to take a theft from a vehicle report and drove straight to the address after the shift briefing. The victim of the crime met him at his car and told Matt that he was a retired Cincinnati cop. The victim handed Matt a sheet of paper containing all of the information that Matt would need to complete the report, including serial numbers and values for each of the items taken. Matt told the retired cop that he would make sure the Police Pawn Shop squad got the information in case the items were pawned.

Matt stopped and picked up coffee and then went to a bank parking lot to enter the information into the police computer. He had not called communications to clear the call so that he would be able to enjoy his coffee, since the report was not officially done. He was almost finished with the report when he heard two cars receive a radio run to an address on his beat. The call was reference a mentally ill male waving a sword in the rear of an apartment building less than half a block away from Matt's location. Matt threw his coffee out of the window and was at the location in less than thirty seconds. He turned into the long driveway along the side of the building, not thinking to notify communications that he was at the location of the call. He drove slowly back the driveway seeing the graffiti on the wall of the multi-story building. When he got to the end of the building, it opened into a parking area for the residents. Matt saw a black male in his twenties standing near the dumpster. The male was swinging the sword wildly as if in some mortal battle. Matt put the cruiser in park and got out of the car. He had just closed the driver's door when the male came running at him at full speed swinging the sword.

As the subject got closer Matt instinctively drew his gun and fired two shots at the suspect. The explosions actually scared Matt because he did not realize that his gun was in his hand. Matt watched in horror as the man's legs gave out and, almost in slow motion, he dropped to the ground. At almost the same time Matt heard an officer screaming into the radio, "SHOTS FIRED, SHOTS FIRED AT MY LOCATION!" Matt turned to see three cops running down the driveway toward him with their guns drawn. Matt approached the now crumpled figure and attempted to kick the sword out of the man's hand, but it didn't budge. Matt reached down and grabbed the blade of the sword which cut deeply into his right palm and four fingers. The sword had been honed down to a razor sharp edge and Matt was gushing blood onto the pavement. The only thing that Matt could think was that his blood was now contaminating the crime scene. One of the cops ran back to Matt's cruiser and popped open the trunk to get the first aid kit while another called for a paramedic unit for an officer injured. The transmitting officer also broadcast an officer involved shooting and called for a supervisor and detectives. The officer with first aid kit wrapped Matt's hand in gauze to slow the bleeding.

Two paramedics were in the grocery store picking up items because it was their turn to cook lunch for the firehouse. They were returning to their unit when the call went out for a police officer down. They threw the food in the back of the unit and drove madly to get to the police officer. One paramedic worked to professionally wrap Matt's injured hand, while the other determined that the suspect was, in fact, dead. A Lieutenant arrived and told the medics to get Matt to the hospital immediately. As Matt was being loaded onto a stretcher, he heard the residents screaming things like, "The cop shot him down like a dog," and "Murderer."

The life squad was just leaving as Captain Newhall arrived at the scene, with the Interim Police Chief and his two Assistant Chiefs arriving moments later. The four men walked back the driveway to the parking lot where a crowd was beginning to gather and others were hanging out of their apartment windows watching the chaos below.

The Lieutenant told the commanders that there was not a lot of information available because the officer involved in the shooting had suffered a serious hand wound attempting to remove the military style sword from the suspect's hand.

The Interim Chief returned to the sidewalk that was now filled with media people. The media ran up with microphones in hand and the Chief gave an impromptu press conference. He told the media people that police had responded to an anonymous 9-1-1 call indicating a man was brandishing a sword in the rear parking area. He told reporters that the officer involved in the shooting had been taken to University of Cincinnati Medical Center with a hand injury suffered while trying to remove the sword from the suspect's hand and that the officer had not yet been able to be interviewed to provide further details as to what happened.

The Chief returned to the shooting site and ordered the Lieutenant to find out where Matt lived and send an officer to notify family and transport them to UC Hospital.

Matt arrived at the hospital and was surprised to see two nurses and a doctor standing at the rear doors of the squad. The doctor used a small flashlight to check his eyes and asked him if he was in any pain.

Matt told the doctor that his hand was throbbing and he felt weak from the loss of blood. The doctor and the nurses followed the medics inside the hospital, where Matt was taken into a treatment room.

The first thing the doctor did was cut open the well wrapped dressing around Matt's injured hand. He told Matt that tests would have to be run to determine what, if any, ligament or tendon damage had been done. Matt asked the people there if any of them had a camera to take pictures of the wound for evidence. One of the nurses made a call to University of Cincinnati Police asking for a camera to be brought over. A University police detective arrived a few minutes later with a crime scene kit and took several pictures of the wound. The detective told Matt that the pictures would be sent to the Homicide Unit. The doctor gave Matt a shot which would numb the pain and knock Matt out so the hand could be inspected.

Back at the scene, things were getting really chaotic, as the crowd was growing into a frenzy over the shooting. The Chief called in the Community Initiative to Reduce Violence staff to attempt to tamper down the high emotions. CIRV is a city program staffed by former felons and gang-bangers, who can effectively relate to the people on their own terms. The statements obtained from the first officers on the scene really did not shed much light on what had transpired, and the civilian witnesses were of not much help either. The Chief returned to again brief the media on what was known, which was very little, and promised a news conference at eleven o'clock the next morning.

A District One officer was told to go to Matt's apartment and take his mother to University Hospital. The officer stood outside the building and rang the buzzer of Matt's apartment. When he heard Matt's mother ask who was there, he told her that he was a Cincinnati Police officer and needed to talk to her. She demanded to know what he wanted, but the officer told her that he needed to get inside to explain why he was there. She finally pushed the buzzer allowing him entry into the building and was waiting at the apartment door when he got off of the elevator. The officer was careful choosing his words as he told her that Matt had been involved in a shooting and had been taken to the hospital with a non life threatening wound to his hand, emphasizing the non life threatening.

Matt's mom was already grabbing her purse and keys as the officer explained that he would take her to the hospital and remain with her until she was ready for him to bring her back home. When they arrived at the waiting room, there were already a group of uniform and plainclothes cops milling around. The officer walked up to a nurse and told her that he had brought the officer's mother to the hospital and to find the doctor who treated Matt so she could hear firsthand his condition.

The nurse returned a few minutes later with the Director of Emergency medicine for UC Hospital who told Matt's mom that her son had suffered a laceration to his right hand and fingers that would require surgery to repair tendons and ligaments, but that he was resting comfortably in a room and was sleeping due to medication. She was told that as soon as he awakened, they would take her to him. The officer assigned to her suggested that they go down to the cafeteria and get some food because someone would contact him by radio if they were not in the waiting room.

Matt awoke in a bit of a daze, having no clue the time or where he was. He looked around and realized that he was in a private room at the hospital and that his right hand was bandaged so that it was immobilized. Matt really needed to use the bathroom so he pushed the alert button to call for a nurse. In mere moments a nurse rushed into the room and he told her he needed to use the bathroom. The nurse offered to get a bedpan and help him use it, but Matt told her he just needed help getting to the bathroom and he would take care of actually going. The nurse helped him to his feet and braced him for the walk. He shut the door and realized that he had been dressed in a hospital gown wearing only his underwear. It was a strange situation because he could not use his right hand to slide his underwear out of the way so that he could urinate and he had to use his left hand to hold it while he peed. After some consternation, he re-opened the door and had the nurse help him back to bed.

Matt asked the nurse where his gun belt and uniform were and she responded that his gun belt and bulletproof vest had been taken by detectives from the Homicide Unit. She also told Matt that his mother was in a waiting area and offered to get her for him.

The nurse brought Matt's mom into the room and he could see that she had been crying. Matt tried to re-assure her that he was fine, but that the doctor wanted him kept overnight because of the drugs they used to sedate him. Matt asked how she had gotten to the hospital and she told him a police officer had come to the apartment and brought her there. Matt told his mom that, if she needed a ride home, she should call the police department and they would send a car to pick her up. She smiled and told Matt the Police Chief had ordered the officer to remain with her until she was ready to return home and that, in fact, there were like twenty cops in the waiting room that she had left. She went on to say that the Chief and two Captains had just left when the nurse came and got her.

She kissed Matt on the cheek and told him to rest and she would see him when he got home tomorrow. Matt was feeling groggy from the meds and fell asleep within moments after his mom left the room. Matt fell into a deep rem sleep and began re-living the incident in a frame-by-frame setting. In the dream he saw himself drawing the gun from the holster, and the fire shooting out of the barrel. He saw the two projectiles leave the barrel and pierce the man's chest and the blood drip out of the wounds. He saw the blank stare on the man's face as his legs caved underneath and the look of a man who knew he was about to die.

Nurses came running into his room from all directions after hearing blood-curdling screams emanating from Matt's room. Matt awoke sweating and short of breath from the dream he had just experienced.

***

Matt was awakened by a doctor who specialized in hand wounds. The doctor told Matt that there was some damage to his right hand, but the extent would not be apparent for a few days. Matt was being released from the hospital but would have to return in a week to have the dressing changed. They would, at that time, determine whether the hand would require surgery or whether it would repair itself. Matt was also given painkillers in case the hand started to hurt.

Matt was embarrassed when he was unable to dress himself and the nurse had to help him put on his pants. They put his uniform shirt in a grocery bag so no one would see him leaving.

The nurse told Matt that they had arranged to move him into another building where a police car was waiting to take him home because there was a flood of media at the front entrance. Matt balked when they told him he had to ride in a wheelchair, but was too groggy and weak to put up any kind of a fight. He was wheeled through the maze of the hospital to a side entrance where a cruiser was sitting in wait. The cop drove Matt home and Matt realized that his house keys were still on his duty belt. Matt called his mom from his cell phone and had her buzz him into the building. The cop demanded to follow Matt all the way to his apartment door just as a precaution. Matt extended his left hand to shake and thank the officer for his help and went into his apartment.

When his mom had returned home the night before, the first thing she did was set the cable television DVR to record the two ten o'clock and two eleven o'clock news broadcasts so Matt could watch them if he chose. When Matt walked in the door she hugged him tightly and told him about the news broadcasts and that the Police Chief had scheduled an eleven o'clock briefing that was going to be broadcast live. She fixed him bacon and eggs for breakfast which he had extreme difficulty trying to eat with his left hand, his right being totally immobilized. His mom made the eggs into a sandwich and cut it in half to make it easier for him to eat since he could eat the slices of bacon using only his left hand.

Matt laid down on the couch and watched the four news broadcasts, grimacing as the reporters interviewed people who called him a murderer. One black woman told the reporter that, even though the guy had a sword, it was not a good enough reason and that the cop just wanted to kill a black man. Others questioned why it was necessary to shoot the suspect when the cop had a Taser and a nightstick. The civil rights activists expressed outrage over the shooting and demanded the officer be fired and charged with Murder.

The press briefing was held in the conference room of District One station and the Chief, his two Assistant Chiefs and the Commander of District Three were sitting behind a long table with microphones in front of them. The Chief said that the information available was sketchy because the officer involved had not yet been interviewed and was released from the hospital early this morning. He went on to reiterate that the officer responded to a 9-1-1 call of a man with a sword and pointed to the sword, which was lying on the table, still showing Matt's blood on it. The Chief picked up the sword by the handle and an Assistant Chief took a sheet of paper and lightly ran it across the blade of the sword slicing the paper into two even pieces. The Chief told the press that the sword had been professionally sharpened to a razor sharp edge. A reporter asked the Chief if he was prepared to release the name of the officer involved, but the Chief politely declined "at this time." There were other questions about the witness statements that the officer was never in danger, but the Chief told the media that the witnesses were being interviewed and the investigation ongoing. Matt saw that there were protestors outside the District One headquarters carrying signs proclaiming Matt to be a murderer and demanding "justice." This was reminiscent of the Thomas shooting that resulted in rioting in the streets of Cincinnati in 2001.

Matt turned the television off and decided to check his voicemails. The first message was from Liza, who wanted to make sure he was okay. Matt called her and the first thing she told him was not to speak to anyone about the specifics of the incident and to call the FOP to have them get him an attorney. The second voicemail was from Captain Newhall, who said he called to make sure that Matt was okay and to tell Matt that he would be on Injured with Pay (IWP) status, but that he would not be able to return to work until he had been cleared by the department psychologist as well. The third voicemail was from the Homicide detective assigned to investigate, who told Matt that, as soon as he felt well enough, they needed to meet to go over what had transpired.

Matt telephoned the FOP Lodge and told the secretary that he needed to obtain legal counsel. The secretary told Matt that the President of the FOP had already contacted a criminal attorney who would go to the interview at Homicide with Matt. She told Matt that he would be receiving a call from Timothy Cusher, an attorney who has been practicing criminal law for almost forty years. Matt was feeling really tired and drained, so he decided to take a nap before doing the things he needed to get done.

Matt fell into a deep sleep and once again re-lived the incident in the same frame-by-frame manner that he had done at the hospital. He scared his mother into almost having a heart attack when he woke screaming and sweating profusely. Matt knew that seeing the psychologist had to be a top priority because he was unsure how often this vivid recall would continue. Matt called the office of Dr. James Don to schedule his appointment. The receptionist asked Matt if he felt it was an emergency or whether she could schedule him in a few days. Matt thought deeply for a moment because of the nightmares, but told the receptionist that whenever the doctor had an opening was fine. She scheduled him for the next day at one-thirty in the afternoon. Matt called the Homicide detective next and scheduled a nine o'clock meeting the next day at the CIS office. His next call was to Cusher to tell him about the appointment. Cusher assured Matt he would be there and to not say anything about the incident to anyone unless he was present.

CHAPTER TWENTY-TWO

Matt walked from his apartment over to the CIS unit which was only a few blocks away. He arrived fifteen minutes early and was greeted by all the cops who told him they were glad he was okay. The lead investigator walked out of the back and went to shake hands with Matt, but then had to switch hands because of the bandage on Matt's right hand. Matt smiled sheepishly and told the detective that it was an easy mistake to make and the two laughed. Matt told the detective that the FOP had gotten him an attorney who told him not to talk about the incident until the attorney was present which would be at nine o'clock. The detective took Matt back to where the coffee pot was located and the two chatted about the seriousness of the injury to Matt's hand. The front desk officer announced that Matt's attorney was at the front desk and the detective went up to meet him. When the three were together, Cusher asked the detective for a private room for him to confer with his client. The detective took them to an interview room and showed Cusher that the audio and video equipment were turned off. He told Cusher to call his four digit line when they were ready for him.

Cusher told Matt to walk him through everything that happened. Matt painstakingly went step-by-step from the time he heard the call until the shooting happened. Cusher listened intently, writing notes on a legal pad as they went along. The first question Cusher asked is why there was no radio communication between Matt and the dispatcher. Matt knew that Cusher had done his homework and explained that he was completing the theft report and was so close to the call that he simply did not get around to it and that the situation escalated so quickly that Matt never had an opportunity to use the radio. Cusher asked if Matt had considered any other force option before resorting to his firearm and Matt's response was that he didn't realize he had drawn his gun and fired until the incident was over.

Cusher called the direct line and the detective came into the room. He activated the audio and video and asked Matt to walk him through exactly what had transpired. Matt told the detective how he came to be in the bank parking lot and how he had just gotten out of his cruiser when the man charged him flailing the sword. The detective advised Matt that the civilian witnesses were providing a different version of the events that happened, at which point Cusher terminated the interview telling the detective he wanted to review those statements and that they would need to re-schedule the rest of the interview. The detective understood that Cusher was protecting his client's interests and told Cusher he would have the statements by mid-afternoon.

As the two stood outside CIS, Cusher said he had a bad feeling about the outcome of this case based upon what he had heard so far. That sent a sense of fear into Matt's heart because he knew that he had done what was necessary to protect his own life. Matt told Cusher about the meeting with the psychologist, and was told not to worry about it because anything that was said was protected under the doctor/patient doctrine. Cusher offered Matt a ride home, but Matt wanted to walk back and digest everything that was happening so quickly.

Matt called Dawn to see if she would be able to come pick him and his mother up so that they could retrieve his car from District Three. She told him she would meet him in half an hour. Matt called his mom to meet him downstairs so she could drive his car back to the apartment.

Matt's mom demanded that she drive him to his appointment to see the psychologist. She took along a book to read while he met with Dr. Don. Dr. Don came into the waiting room and Matt introduced him to his mother. They went into the back and discussed the nature of the injury to Matt's hand. Matt took the Dr. through exactly what had happened and about the nightmares he had experienced at the hospital and again at home. Dr. Don told Matt that the nightmares were normal because of the nature of the traumatic incident. He said that they would probably continue for a period of time, but that they would become less and less intense. Don told Matt that the taking of a human life violates the basic tenets of a human being and the mind would have continuing difficulty processing the details of the incident. He went on to say that only time would help Matt sort it out and move on. They scheduled a second session for a week later and Matt was told to call immediately if he needed to. Matt felt a bit better that his reactions were not unusual. He also decided to call Thomas, the cop who he went with on the boat because Thomas had also killed a suspect.

***

The six o'clock news had a press release giving Matt's name to the media. The press release stated that Matt had been with the department for just over eighteen months and had no disciplinary actions in his personnel file. Matt had known that his name would be released to the public at some point, but it still scared him that it was now known by all that he had killed another man.

Matt took a pain pill to help him sleep through the night and did not experience the horror of the recurring dream. His cell phone ringing in the morning woke him and the caller was from District One. The officer told Matt that, somehow his home address had gotten out, and there were protestors outside of his apartment building. Matt walked to the window and saw eight people carrying signs demanding his arrest and calling him a murderer. He also saw two marked cruisers parked on the other side of the street. The District One cop told Matt that the two cars would remain as long as the protestors were there.

Matt's mom told him that she needed to grocery shop and would be back soon. Matt's original thought was to not tell his mom about the protestors outside, but this was a game changer. He told his mom to ignore the protestors and not acknowledge that she knew him. He told her that there were two cops outside and that, if they gave her any grief, to motion to them for help. Matt's mom was approached by a black woman carrying a sign proclaiming Matt a murderer and demanded to know if she knew Matt. Matt's mom ignored the woman and walked to the car without further discussion. As she was walking back to the door the woman became more pushy demanding to know if she knew Matt. Out of the corner of her eye, Matt's mom saw the two cops get out of their cruisers and she motioned them back to their cars and entered the building without incident.

Over the next two days Matt saw the same number of protestors each day, but the faces were different. That led Matt to believe that this was some kind of coordinated effort rather than just some pissed off people.

Matt received a call from Cusher telling him that Cusher had seen the protestors outside Matt's building on the news. Cusher said he had reviewed the witness statements and that they were incoherent and inconsistent. Cusher told Matt he had scheduled a meeting with the detective, but that Matt did not need to be present. Cusher also said that he would be able to review all of the crime scene photos and evidence collected at the scene and would call Matt as soon as the meeting was over.

Cusher called Matt to tell him that all of the evidence had been turned over to the Hamilton County Prosecutor by the Police Department and that the case would be presented to a Grand Jury the next morning. Cusher assured Matt that this was normal procedure and nothing to be alarmed about and that it was highly unlikely that the Grand Jury would come back with an indictment. The thought of being indicted caused Matt's stomach to churn and his attorney's assurances provided little solace.

The next day the Hamilton County Prosecutor held a news conference that was also carried live by the local stations, announcing that a Grand Jury had declined to indict the officer involved in the shooting. With the Police Chief at his side and the sword lying on a table in front of them, the Prosecutor told the reporters that the sharpened sword presented an immediate and imminent danger to the officer and that the force used by the officer was both reasonable and necessary. Matt felt a sense of total relief at hearing that and his mother sat and cried.

Matt received congratulatory calls from Liza and Dawn. He also received a call from Captain Newhall telling him that the psychologist had cleared him to return to duty as soon as his hand healed up.

After five long days, the protestors outside magically disappeared. Luckily, it was on the same day as Matt's appointment to have the dressing changed at UC Medical Center. The doctor told Matt that the wound was healing fine and that surgery did not appear to be necessary. The doctor said that Matt would be cleared for light duty within a week and should be able to return to full duty within two weeks if he completed the exercises on the paper that he would be given.

Matt went home with the less restrictive bandage and immediately worked to strengthen his hand doing the exercises on the list. Three days later Matt called Captain Newhall and told him that he had been approved to return to work on light duty. The Captain told him to report for his normal shift the next day and he would be assigned to the front desk. Matt was less than ecstatic over the prospect of riding a desk, but anything would be a marked improvement over the claustrophobia he was feeling sitting around the apartment.

Matt also needed to get his gun belt back from the Homicide Unit. He called the lead investigator who told Matt that he would bring it over personally. The detective arrived at Matt's apartment and told Matt he was glad that Matt had been exonerated in the shooting.

Matt arrived at District Three for his first shift back to back-slapping and handshakes from all the other cops. He soon identified a problem he was going to encounter because the job called for a lot of writing and Matt was having difficulty closing his right hand around a pen. Using a blank piece of paper, Matt would scribble whatever he needed to write and then slowly write the information onto an official document. This was going to be a tedious time. He felt lucky that cops would come by and ask what he wanted them to pick up for his dinner.

Matt was into his third day on the desk when two men in business suits entered the public entrance to the District. The two identified themselves as Special Agents from the FBI here to see Officer Matt Miles. Matt told them he was Matt Miles and asked what he could do for them. They said they needed to talk to him about his shooting, and needed a private space. Matt called a supervisor who took over the desk while Matt led the two agents to an interview room that was vacant.

The one agent introduced himself as Danny Sabitini and said that the FBI was investigating a Civil Rights complaint in the shooting Matt had been involved in. The agent told Matt that he had joined the FBI from being a street cop in Baltimore and that the investigation was a mere formality. The other agent sat quietly and Matt had a gut feeling that there was more to the story than the agent was letting on.

Matt asked Sabitini if he was going to read Matt his Miranda rights since a Civil Rights beef was a criminal matter. Sabatini replied that he did not believe that was going to be necessary but the other agent reached into a folder he was carrying a brought out a written waiver form for Miranda. Matt took one look at the form and told the two Feds that he would not waive his right to have an attorney present and asked if he was free to leave. Sabitini asked Matt for the name and number of his attorney and the two men walked out of the room without saying another word. The Miranda form was still laying on the table as they left.

The next morning Matt received a phone call from Tim Cusher telling him the FBI had contacted him about the Civil Rights complaint and he had told the agent that, under no circumstances, would he allow Matt to be interviewed.

Matt reported for his shift and was told that he needed to leave immediately and report to the Chief's office. Matt drove to District One and went to the Police Chief's office, where he was told the Chief would be with him in a few minutes. The secretary motioned for Matt to go in and the Interim Chief told him to have a seat. The Chief said he had received a call from the FBI advising they were conducting a criminal investigation of a potential Civil Rights violation and that it was the policy of the Police Department to suspend the police powers of officers being investigated. Matt would have to surrender his badge and gun pending the outcome, but would still report for work and be paid by the department. Matt would be assigned to the Telephone Crime Reporting Unit in District One. TCRU takes reports of minor crimes over the telephone and is known as the Penalty Box for miscreant cops. Matt put his badge and his gun on the Chief's desk and was told to take the day off and report to TCRU at eight o'clock in the morning. Matt would be back to working an eight hour shift five days a week.

Matt drove home and immediately called Cusher on his cell phone. He related what had transpired and Cusher warned him to be prepared for a Federal indictment because the Justice Department had a history of indicting innocent cops.
Matt spent the next two weeks taking complaints over the telephone and was bored to death. The thought of an impending indictment by the Feds caused him to have sleeping and eating problems, and his life was literally a train wreck.

Matt was sitting at his desk when the Police Chief's secretary walked up and told him the Chief needed to see him immediately. Matt walked into the Chief's office and was told that the FBI had called him to tell him that a Federal Grand Jury had indicted him for the

Civil Rights violation under Section 1983 of the United States Code. The Chief told Matt that he had until four o'clock in the afternoon to turn himself in to the FBI at their office in the Federal Building in downtown Cincinnati. Matt would be suspended without pay pending the outcome of the case.

Matt left the Chief's office in total shock and dismay, He called Cusher's office and told the attorney he needed to turn himself in. Cusher told Matt to meet him on the steps of the Federal Building at three-thirty and they would go in together. Matt drove home so that he could personally tell his mother and not let her hear it on the evening news.

CHAPTER TWENTY-THREE

Matt walked over to the Federal Building and found Cusher standing on the steps awaiting his arrival. They went up to the FBI office where Cusher told the desk agent that Matt was there to surrender himself. Two agents came out from the back and escorted Matt directly into a Federal Magistrate's office. The Magistrate read the charge against Matt which alleged that he unlawfully caused the death of Harold Motz, a human being, while acting under color of law in violation of United States Code Section 1983. The magistrate set Matt's bond at two hundred and fifty thousand dollars and ordered the US Marshals to take him into custody. A screaming match erupted between Cusher and the Magistrate, stopping only when the Magistrate threatened to incarcerate Cusher for Contempt of Court. Matt was handcuffed and taken out a rear door, then down a hallway to an elevator. The elevator went to the underground garage where Matt was placed in the back of an unmarked white van with no windows.

Matt could only see out of the front window of the van as it turned south on Walnut Street. When it passed Fifth Street which runs east and would be the way to the Hamilton County Jail, Matt asked the passenger where he was being transported to. The reply he got was that he was being taken to the Boone County, Kentucky Detention

Center, some forty miles south of Cincinnati. Matt asked why and was told that Boone County had a contract to hold Federal prisoners.

Cusher stormed out of the Magistrate's room and called Matt's mom. He told her to meet him on the street in front of her apartment and to bring her checkbook. Cusher took Matt's mom to a bank where she got a cashier's check for the bail amount. They then drove to the Hamilton County Justice Center to post Matt's bond and get him released. The Deputy Clerk of Courts looked at Cusher like he was crazy and told the attorney no one by that name had been brought to the Jail.

Cusher and Matt's mom drove back to the Federal Building and Cusher stormed into the US Marshal Service office demanding to know where Matt was being held. The female at the desk told Cusher that Matt had been processed into the Boone County Jail within the past half hour. When Cusher asked why Boone County he was told that it was where the Magistrate had ordered him taken. Cusher stormed out of that office and was on his way to confront the Magistrate when he stopped, changed direction and dragged Matt's mom to the chambers of a Federal Judge whose husband happened to be another prominent Cincinnati attorney. The two entered the courtroom and Cusher told the bailiff that he needed to see the Judge for an emergency situation. The bailiff disappeared into the

Judge's chambers, but was back within ten seconds motioning for them to come in.

The door had no sooner closed when Cusher began explaining what had occurred. The Judge had a scowl on her face as she hit the intercom button and told her bailiff to get the Magistrate into her chambers ten minutes ago. A few minutes later the Magistrate entered the Judge's chambers wearing a smirk until he saw Cusher and Matt's mom sitting in the corner. The door had no sooner closed when she began screaming at the Magistrate as if he were a four year old child who had been caught playing with matches. She was ordering a change in Matt's bond to Own Recognizance, which means he would return on his word. The screaming ended when she ordered the Magistrate out of her chambers.

Matt was brought into the booking area of the jail where he was ordered to empty his pockets and then searched by a deputy jailer. The US Marshals signed over custody of Matt and he was escorted to a private area and ordered to strip naked. He was told to bend over and spread the cheeks of his ass and then cough. The deputy jailer put on a latex glove and shoved a finger into Matt's ass to make sure he was not carrying contraband. Because Matt had a bandage still on his hand, the jail nurse had to be called to cut it off to make sure there was nothing in it. She re-wrapped the wound and told Matt that it appeared to be healing nicely. Matt was told to put his underwear and tee shirt back on and given a bright orange jumpsuit with the words BOONE COUNTY JAIL emblazoned on the back.

Matt was then escorted down a hallway and placed in a one-person cell in an area that appeared to be otherwise empty. The deputy told Matt that word was all over the jail that a cop had been brought in and they needed to isolate him for his own safety. Matt sat on the hard cot in the cell with his head in his lap hoping that this was just a bad dream he was having.

The Judge picked up her phone and called the Marshal Service ordering them to go pick up Matt and bring him to her chambers. She told the person on the other end of the phone that, if Matt was wearing a jail jumpsuit, people would be searching for new jobs the next day. She told Cusher that the process might take a couple of hours and that they were welcome to wait in her chambers or she would call Cusher the minute he was brought in. Cusher told the Judge they needed to re-deposit the bail check into the bank before it closed.

A deputy jailer walked by Matt's cell and snickered about having a Cincinnati cop as a prisoner. Matt asked him what his problem was and the jailer told Matt a Cincinnati cop had given him a speeding ticket two weeks earlier. Matt put his head back into his hands and just ignored the clown. Another jailer stopped and told Matt that dinner would be served in about twenty minutes, but Matt probably would not like the food.

Matt's plate had just been passed through the cell door when the loudspeaker announced that he was to be brought to the booking area immediately. Now Matt was really confused as to what he could have possibly done. Matt was taken back into the private area and handed his street clothes and told to put them on. When he was dressed he was escorted to two US Marshals wearing raid jackets. He was handcuffed and taken to a Ford Crown Victoria where he was seat-belted in on the passenger side rear seat and a US Marshal sat to his left. Matt asked what the HELL was going on and was told that he was to be taken to the chambers of a Federal Judge.

The Judge was seated at her desk when the handcuffed Matt was brought in. She immediately ordered the handcuffs be removed and told the Marshals she did not need them any longer. The two Marshals looked astonished but turned and left the chambers without speaking a word. The Judge looked at Matt and told him to have a seat. She picked up her phone and told the person on the other end of the line that Matt was there and they could come get him.

The Judge apologized profusely for the actions of the Magistrate and told him his mom and Cusher were on their way to get him. She pushed a form in front of him that stated he would return for Court which he immediately signed. Matt let out a sigh of relief knowing he would be sleeping in his own bed tonight.

CHAPTER TWENTY-FOUR

As the three walked out of the Federal Building Cusher advised Matt that he would need to appear before a Federal Judge to enter his plea of not guilty. The date for that would be set by the Court in the next few days. He also told Matt that it was likely to become a media circus reminiscent of the Rodney King case in California. He told Matt that they would meet at the courthouse and Matt was to keep walking, looking straight ahead and saying nothing to anyone. Cusher said he would answer any questions the media people had.

On the day of the arraignment, Matt and his mom made the walk from the apartment to the Federal Courthouse. As Cusher had predicted, media trucks were everywhere as were protestors carrying signs calling Matt a "killer" and a "murderer." Media people and cameras walked to the steps yelling questions at Matt, who followed his counsel's advice and ignored the circus around him. Once they were able to reach the doors of the Courthouse, the media people had to back away as cameras are not permitted inside of a Federal Courthouse. The hearing took only minutes to complete. The Judge, who appeared to be in his seventies, asked Matt if he understood the charge against him. Matt replied simply, "Yes, your Honor." The Judge then asked how he wanted to plead and Matt quietly, but firmly, replied, "not guilty, your Honor." The Judge set a pre-trial conference for three weeks later that would be held in his chambers. Cusher presented the US Attorney and the Judge with a Motion for Discovery demanding all of the evidence to be presented by the government and their list of witnesses that they would be calling.

Before the three left the Courthouse Cusher set up a strategy meeting for the next afternoon at his office, which also was in the downtown area where they would sit down and look at the evidence and choose a direction to fight the charge. Cusher warned that this was likely to be a very lengthy case because the government would want to wear Matt down to get him to take a plea bargain. He went on to say that is was a good bet that they would make Matt an offer at the pre-trial that was coming up.

Matt went home and jumped onto the internet to search for answers to the charges. He started with the Sixth Circuit Court of Appeals, which is based in Cincinnati and has jurisdiction over all of the Federal Courts in Ohio, Kentucky, Tennessee and Michigan. He typed in the search parameters "1983" and found dozens of cases involving Civil Rights actions, but none of them involved criminal prosecutions of police officers. He next went to the US Supreme Court site and, using the same search criteria, found a number of cases. One criminal case from 1989 that originated in Charlotte, North Carolina came up and Matt clicked on the link. The case, titled <u>Graham v Connor,</u> established a gold standard for determining whether force used by police was reasonable. Matt found the wording for the standard which said that the test of reasonableness would be answered in a simple question. What would a reasonable police officer do in a like situation?

Matt printed the decision and placed it in a folder he had created to help in his defense.

***

Matt showed up at Cusher's office and the two began looking at the evidence the Cincinnati Police had collected from the scene. As he looked through the pictures, Matt felt himself re-live again the face of the man as he crumpled to the pavement from the two gunshot wounds to the chest. After looking at all the pictures, Matt realized that the pictures the UC Police had taken of his hand were not in the file. He told Cusher that and was told to wait and see if the Feds had them when they finally received the discovery request.

Matt reached into his folder and laid the Graham decision on the table. Cusher picked it up and started reading the facts and the decision of the Court and a smile came to his face. He told Matt that he would draw up a Motion to Dismiss and they would drop it on the government at the pre-trial conference.

Matt went home and sat at the dinner table with his mom to discuss the next steps of their lives. Matt was considering finding a job to keep him occupied since money was not an issue. He had saved up a substantial sum from his job and his mother was set for life with the insurance payment and the money from the sale of their home in California.

Matt's mom suggested that Matt go back to school and work toward his Masters Degree or, better yet, go to law school. Matt had never considered the possibility of becoming an attorney, but the challenge was something to be considered. Matt would apply to get into the prestigious Xavier University School of Law and see what happens.

Matt contacted UCLA to obtain a transcript of his attendance and was told it would be mailed out to him. His 3.8 grade point average should qualify him to be admitted to the Law School. He checked the mail every day, just as he had when awaiting the results of his application for the Cincinnati Police, and it finally arrived.

Matt went to the admissions office at Xavier and met with a counselor. They completed the necessary paperwork to submit, but Matt wanted to be up front with the school and told the counselor that he was currently under Federal Indictment. The look on the counselor's face told Matt that this was likely to be a major stumbling block to overcome.

It took almost two weeks, but Matt finally got a letter from the school stating that his application had been declined, but it gave no reason(s) for the decision. Matt contacted Xavier School of Law and asked for a meeting with the Dean of the Law School. Matt was told that the deadline for acceptance was only two weeks away and that the Dean would be able to give him one hour the next day. Matt thanked the receptionist and said he would be there on time.

Matt's mom picked out his wardrobe for the meeting that consisted of a conservative gray suit, a pale blue dress shirt and a medium blue tie. Matt took a black portfolio folder containing his transcript in order to enhance his professional demeanor. The Dean was sitting at his desk and looked impressed when he first saw Matt walk into his office. Matt sat in the chair directly in front of the desk and leaned a bit forward to exhibit body language of power.

Matt handed the Dean his UCLA transcript and the Dean leaned back into his chair to read it. Matt had to mask the internal churning he was feeling and show a calm and confident persona. The Dean looked at Matt and said that, although his transcript was impressive, the fact that he was under indictment for a crime made his acceptance into the school very doubtful.

Matt respectfully argued that his indictment was the direct result of an action related to his job and that the government lacked a credible case because of the Graham standard. The Dean's eyes showed a definite interest and Matt continued that his actions in the unfortunate event were both reasonable and necessary, and that he had no doubt that he would prevail at trial. The Dean asked Matt to talk specifically about the US Supreme Court's ruling in the Graham case and Matt showed a clear understanding of the ruling. The Dean explained that a criminal conviction would preclude Matt from obtaining a license to practice law in Ohio and Matt told him he fully understood that. The Dean said that he would present Matt's case to the selection committee and they would make a decision prior to the deadline for admission. He gave Matt a strong handshake that actually caused pain in Matt's injured right hand. The Dean saw the grimace in Matt's face and apologized, but the smile on Matt's face was profound because he now felt the Dean was going to be on his side.

***

Cusher and Matt appeared for the pre-trial conference held in the Judge's chambers. The representative from the US Attorney looked like a ninth grader on a field trip to a courtroom. His smug persona gave rise to the belief that he had gotten the job because his father was a large contributor to the Obama Presidential campaign. The young prosecutor told Cusher that the government was prepared to offer Matt a one year prison sentence in return for a guilty plea which brought a wry smile to Cusher's face.

Cusher handed the Judge a Motion for Dismissal and tossed a copy onto the lap of the kid attorney. The prosecutor sat and silently read the pleading, showing a pained look as he read that the Court was obligated to follow the Supreme Court ruling set forth in <u>Graham v Connor</u>. The prosecutor looked at the Judge and claimed that the government had thirty days to file its response and that the Court could not rule on it until then. The Judge, who also quietly read the content of the motion, looked up from the filing and announced that he would withhold his ruling until the first day of trial. The Judge set a trial date just over eight months away and the conference was over.

As they left the Courthouse, Cusher told Matt that they had neither won nor lost. Matt questioned why the Judge would not rule until the trial started and Cusher told him that they could not appeal an adverse ruling on the motion until the Judge actually made a ruling and that it was a stalling tactic to give the government time to actually develop a case against Matt. Cusher said that likely nothing would occur until days or weeks before the trial date and that Matt should just go about his daily business and not worry. There would be more than enough time to stress out as the trial date approached.

CHAPTER TWENTY-FIVE

Three days later Matt received his letter of acceptance to law school and celebrated with by taking his mother to Ruth Chris Steak House on the Banks. He went to the school and signed up for eighteen credit hours the first semester, over the strong objections of the registrar since twelve credit hours is considered a full time student. Matt felt comfortable handling the heavy load which would complete the three years of study in less than two years.

Matt settled into a regiment of using almost every waking hour staying caught in his coursework. Him mother had found a full time job and moved out of the apartment to allow him the quiet time he so badly needed. He had also begun dating Dawn and the relationship was starting to develop into something serious.

Dawn and Matt had discussed her possibly moving in with him, but there might be an issue that would preclude that from happening. Matt called Cusher and set up a lunch meeting to discuss the problem. Since Matt was under indictment for a felony crime he was precluded by law from being in the possession of a firearm and the fact that Dawn was a police officer would mean that firearms would be in a shared environment. That would put him in constructive possession and potentially complicate his criminal case or cause a new charge to be brought either by a State or Federal prosecution.

After the facts were explained to Matt's attorney, Cusher told Matt that he would contact the supervising prosecutor for the Southern District of Ohio and ask them for their position on the issue and that he would get back to Matt with their response as soon as he got it. They decided to postpone the move because it might complicate her status as a police officer as well.

Matt continued to do his morning runs, stretching the distance of the runs to almost marathon length. The rest of the day would either be spent in the classroom or trying to keep up with the papers that would come due and the tests that he needed to take. The first semester flew by and his lofty goal of eighteen hours was taking its toll. The positive to all this stress was that it left no room for him to worry about the pending criminal action.

Matt was surprised when he made Law Review at the conclusion of his first semester. His instructors were in awe of how he was able to understand the complexities of the law and to make dynamic presentations of whatever position he was chosen to argue.

One of his first instructors hammered home what the instructor called the first rule of law. He told the students, "If you lack the facts to support your position, then you argue the law. If the law does not support your position, then you argue the facts. If neither the facts nor the law support your position, then JUST ARGUE!" Matt typed that onto a form and printed it and posted it above the work station he created at home.

It was coming up on the Christmas holidays and Matt convinced to Dawn to take a week vacation and they would take a trip together. Matt suggested going to the Bahamas where they could soak up some sun and get away from the stressors they both were facing. Dawn had been transferred to District Four and was getting grief from a couple of supervisors that she was romantically involved with a man under indictment. She had a pending grievance that she filed with the FOP but, because Cincinnati had a new Police Chief, it had not been addressed as of yet.

Matt's mom had also found a companion as well and the four would go out for evenings of dinners and shows. Matt really liked the guy, who was a successful business owner of a bicycle shop near the University campus.

Matt and Dawn flew from Cincinnati to Miami where they boarded a cruise ship that would take them to the Bahamas. They spent a lot of time talking about their futures and Matt confided in her that he was considering not returning to the Police when, not if, he was found innocent of the charge. Dawn still loved being a member of the Police Department and had no intention of giving up her career.

As soon as they returned to Cincinnati, Matt signed up for another eighteen credit hours of classes. He had joined a study group that met each week at each of the member's homes to prepare jointly their assignments. Dawn would occasionally also attend because she too was deeply interested in the law. A couple of the study group smoked marijuana, but respected that Dawn and Matt wanted no part of that activity. They would go outside in the cold and snow to partake of their doobie, then return to the group for the continuation of their studies. The second semester for Matt was even more difficult than the first, but Dawn seemed to handle his lack of free time extremely well. She knew that his being immersed in his studies kept him from dwelling on his uncertain future.

At the end of the second semester Matt again made the law review. He was contacted by several prestigious law firms about serving as an intern with them when he reached his third year status. Matt was told that the Dean of the Law School had personally offered a recommendation of him to them and that there might be an employment offer in his future.

As the trial date approached Matt began meeting with Cusher to discuss a strategy. Matt was told that the FOP had set aside seventy thousand dollars for his defense fund, but that would run out if they chose to hire use of force experts to testify that Matt's actions were reasonable and necessary. The government had listed six experts to testify on their side, so a defense strategy would need to offset the unlimited finances that the government could throw into railroading Matt. Matt checked with his mother and was told that money was not a consideration and she would pay for whatever expenses he incurred.

CHAPTER TWENTY-SIX

As Matt, Dawn, his mother and Cusher approached the steps of the Federal Court for the first day of his trial, Matt marveled at how Cusher had predicted a media circus. The networks had reporters out front along with all of the local media and there were a significant number of protestors with signs proclaiming him a killer.

Cameras and microphones and people yelling questions at him at the speed of light surrounded him. As he had done the last time, he looked straight forward and remained totally silent.

The courtroom was paced with spectators and a bailiff had to move people so Dawn and Matt's mom could sit directly behind Matt. The Judge moved up to the bench and asked both parties if they were ready to begin the jury selection. The smug kid prosecutor rose and told the Judge the government was prepared. Cusher rose from his seat and told the Judge that the trial could not begin until the Judge ruled on the defense's Motion to Dismiss and that he would like to be heard on that issue. The Judge, who looked less than happy, told Cusher he could proceed.

Cusher handed the bailiff a copy of <u>Graham v Connor</u> to be handed to the Judge and then placed another copy on the prosecution's table. He told the Judge that he was prepared to amend his witness list to include every sworn member of the Cincinnati Police Department and each would be asked only one question. That question would be, "If a man charged at you with a military sword, would you consider deadly force a reasonable and necessary option?" Next Cusher handed the bailiff seven photographs that had taken of Matt's injured hand by the University of Cincinnati Police Department. Those pictures graphically demonstrated the significant injury that Matt incurred by simply touching the sword.

The Judge ordered both counsel into his chambers and he sat down at his desk. He handed the photographs to the young prosecutor and proclaimed, "Your case was garbage at its inception and it just turned to shit!" The smug little man got a pained look and tried to argue that Matt had alternatives other than the use of deadly force and the case should proceed. A smile came to the old Judge's face as he proclaimed the great cliché', "Son, that dog don't hunt!" He told the attorneys that he would grant the Defendant's Motion to Dismiss and the case was over.

The parties returned to their places and Matt could see the smile on Cusher's face. The Judge ordered Matt and his attorney to stand and then read into the Court record, "This Court grants Defendant's Motion to Dismiss and releases Defendant from the charge against him. Son, you are a free man."

There were immediate gasps from the civil rights activists in the courtroom as Matt's mom and Dawn jumped out of their seats to hug Matt. The four walked out of the courtroom and Cusher stopped them in the hallway. He told Matt that he had no obligation to make any statement to the swarm of media outside, who would have just heard the Judge's ruling. Cusher said he would stand in front of the microphones and tell the world that justice had truly been served. Matt said he would rather that Cusher make any statements and Matt would continue to remain silent.

Matt told the three that he had made a decision not to return to the Police Department and he was going to pursue his degree in law. Cusher cautioned that Matt needed to return for at least one day in order for him to collect the almost one year in salary that he had lost. Cusher told Matt that he would hand deliver the Judgment Entry of the Court to the newly appointed Police Chief along with a letter demanding Matt's back pay and told all of them to go out and celebrate Matt's freedom, and that he would take care of the rest.

Matt stood tall directly behind Cusher as he addressed the hoards of media. He told the media that Matt had served the City of Cincinnati in an exemplary manner and that, although the loss of life is a tragic event, that Matt was protecting the residents of the City as well as defending himself from a dangerous individual.

CHAPTER TWENTY-SEVEN

Matt and Dawn, his mom and her male friend, went to the Montgomery Inn Boathouse to celebrate the end of the case. Montgomery Inn became famous when comedian Bob Hope would have their ribs shipped to his California estate for special events that he would host. They sat at the table and enjoyed the savory ribs and a bottle of champagne. At the end of the meal Matt reached into the right pocket of his jacket and brought out a small box. He opened the box under Dawn's nose and asked her quietly to marry him. Dawn scared the hell out of all the patrons of the restaurant when she jumped to her feet and screamed out, "Of course I will marry you!" There was applause from the full restaurant as Matt and Dawn hugged and kissed.

Matt reported to the Police Chief's office to be returned his badge and his gun. Once he had been officially reinstated, Matt laid an envelope on the Chief's desk. The new Police Chief, who had come to Cincinnati from the Columbus, Ohio Police Department, opened the envelope and read Matt's letter of resignation. Having been reinstated, Matt was now eligible for all of his back pay and he laid the badge back down on the Chief's desk and walked out the door without saying a word.

Matt had seen the good, the bad and the ugly of choosing law enforcement as a profession and he knew that he would be leaving the profession with his head held high and proud that he had chosen it as a career. The lessons learned had made him a better person. It was now time to move on with his life.

As he walked silently down the hallway from the Chief's office, Matt's thoughts were moving at the speed of a runaway freight train and he was having difficulty making sense of anything. He had just given up a career that he had come to love, his fiancé would be moving in with him at the end of the week, and his college course load was taking a toll on him. When the elevator arrived at the first level, Matt instinctively turned to his right to exit via the police employee entrance, but stopped and turned around because he was no longer a Cincinnati cop. He walked up to the door and had to hit on the glass partition to get the desk officer's attention. The knocking also caught the attention of several cops inside the District who stopped what they were doing to watch Matt intently. Matt would not make eye contact with any of the cops as the desk man hit the buzzer to electronically unlock the civilian entrance door. Without looking back, Matt walked out of the District and headed for his car.

Matt knew that he could not go home in this state of mind so he decided to actually tour the Seven Hills of Cincinnati. He pulled the

Mustang out of the Police parking lot for last time and headed east to start his journey. He slowly drove to Mount Adams, then east to Walnut Hills, then west to Mount Auburn. He drove past the University of Cincinnati campus as he headed northwest to College Hill and then west to Mount Airy. He drove southwest into Western Hills and then completed the cycle when he reached Price Hill. He pulled into a drive-thru to get a burger and fries and then slowly drove past the entrance to the apartment building where the shooting occurred. He headed west to Mount Echo Park which overlooks the Ohio River. When he pulled into the park, he was glad that there appeared to be no one there except him.

Matt found a bench that looked down on the river and set his food by his side on the bench. He was slowly eating his sandwich in the glowing sun of the day when he heard the Beach Boys song "Help me Rhonda" coming from his pocket. He didn't even think to look to see the caller id and just said "Hello." The next sound he heard was Dawn screaming, "Where are you and what the fuck happened? I just heard on the news that you quit!" Matt was silent as he tried to find the words to answer his fiancé, and he finally told her he was in the park and trying to sort out all of his thoughts and emotions. She ordered him not to move and that she would be there in five minutes. Matt hung up the phone and went back to his food, but he thought about how his mother would find out and needed to call her. When she answered, he said "Mom, I went in and quit today. I wanted you to hear it first from me, rather than from the news. I will call you later with the details." When he hung up he sat and watched a barge that was moving down the Ohio River at the speed of a sloth, thinking how peaceful it was watching the Ohio River and the Kentucky skyline. He was almost totally wrapped up in the moment when he heard the loud roar of a police interceptor engine getting closer by the second. He turned and watched the park entrance as the marked cruiser came squealing into the road. The police car came to a stop only inches away from the bumper of Matt's Mustang.

Matt did not see the woman who was walking on the path dragging her young son along. He was watching Dawn jump out of the cruiser and run toward him. Dawn sat on the bench and he told her, "I needed to quit, it was the right thing to do. It would have been impossible for me to do the job with the shooting hanging over my head."

Dawn moved over and kissed him causing the young boy to yank on his mother's hand and yell, "Mommy that cop just kissed the guy sitting on the bench!"

The Police radio on dawn's shoulder cracked out a call for a subject being shot. Dawn got a pained look on her face as she told Matt that the shooting was on her beat which she was out of. She ran to her cruiser and left the park with her overhead lights on and siren blasting.

Matt was startled when the woman walked over to him demanding to know what the hell was going on and why the female cop was kissing him. Without thinking, Matt told the woman that he was also a Cincinnati policeman and that the cop was his fiancé. He told her that she had a call to a shooting and that is the reason for the quick exit. The woman just huffed and dragged the child in the other direction.

***

Dawn drove like a madman to get to the call so no one would know that she had left her assigned beat. As she drove onto the dead end street, she saw a male with a gun in his hand standing over a man lying on the ground. She jumped out of the cruiser and drew her 40 caliber sidearm just as the black male holding the gun showed a Cincinnati Police badge in his other hand.

Dawn called for a supervisor and the homicide dicks announcing an off-duty officer involved shooting. The man who was shot was dead on the grass. Dawn looked at the cop and told him, "My fiancé just went through hell over a shooting and you need to keep your mouth shut until you can lawyer up!" The cop looked stunned and replied, "Is Miles your boyfriend?" Dawn just nodded as the paramedics arrived followed by the usual line of police cars.

***

Matt finished his lunch and made sure to clean up the area before leaving. He could go home now that his head was on straight. After parking his car in the garage, he was surprised to see that there were protestors still outside his building, but the marked police car was gone.

He walked past the protestors who did not confront him and went into his apartment. His phone showed sixteen messages, so he hit the play button. The first was from Dawn so he deleted it. The second was from Liza checking to make sure he was okay and he made a mental note to call her back. The next was the Captain of District One telling him that the protection detail had been pulled because the overtime budget had run out. The next was from the Captain of District Three who called to tell him how sorry he was to lose Matt and wishing him well in whatever he decided to do. All but the last call were from other cops wishing him well. The final message was from a female voice who said, "My name is Dania Davison and I am a producer for FOX News. We wanted to know if you would be willing to come to New York to appear on FOX News to tell your story. " Matt called the number that the woman had given, demanding to know how she got his home phone number, and when she refused to tell him he hung up on her.

CHAPTER TWENTY-EIGHT

Matt called Cusher to tell his lawyer that he had resigned from the Police Department, but Cusher said he already knew. Cusher told Matt that he had fielded calls from ABC, CBS, CNN and NBC News asking if Matt would appear on their morning shows. Matt laughed into the phone and told Cusher that the reason there was not a call from FOX is that somehow FOX had gotten his home phone number.

Cusher advised against Matt appearing on network television, but the final decision was Matt's to make. Matt laughed again and told Cusher that he had already gotten his 'fifteen minutes of fame and wanted no part of dealing with the media.

***

Dawn moved her belongings into the apartment and they began planning the wedding while Matt went back to finishing his law degree. Her parents wanted a church wedding with all the bells and whistles which frustrated Matt to tears, but he wisely kept those feelings to himself.

Matt was still a rock star on campus. He was either loved or hated depending upon the viewpoint of the student. As he was leaving a tort class, the instructor called him to the side and told him that the Dean of the Law School wanted to see him as soon as possible. He went directly to the Dean's Office and was directed into the office as soon as the secretary saw him. The Dean told Matt to sit down because the Dean had a favor to ask. Matt looked quizzically as the Dean explained what he needed from Matt.

"Xavier University and the University of Cincinnati hold a moot court each year prior to their basketball matchup which is legendary in Cincinnati. The judges are real judges from the Sixth Circuit Court of Appeals and the losing Dean of Law has to sit on the other school's side of the court wearing their school's colors." For the previous two years, the Dean of Xavier Law School had been humiliated, forced to wear his Xavier blue sweatshirt in the UC cheering section, and he wanted no more of it. The Dean asked Matt to lead the legal team in the moot court case. He would be able to pick his own two co-counsel for the litigation.

Matt thought to himself that he was not doing any favor for the Dean, but that the Dean was bestowing an honor upon him. He immediately accepted and was given five days to name the other two students to be on his team. The only early information that he would be given is that the case was a product liability litigation.

Matt drove home thinking about who would be best suited to be on his team for the moot court. He wanted one person who was a research specialist and the other to be versed in trial litigation. He would listen to the members of his classes to see if anyone stood out over the next few days.

***

Matt had a term paper that was due in less than one week. He had already chosen the topic and had the research lying on the dining room table, but he needed to put it all together quickly and completely. The paper, which he truly believed would be controversial, was titled, "THE POLITICS OF PROSECUTING POLICE OFFICERS." It would be a case study of criminal cases brought by State Prosecutors against police officers involved in on-duty deadly use of force encounters. Matt did not want to only focus on Cincinnati cases, but wanted a national theme to show a pattern.

The first case was out of Granville, Texas and involved a shooting of a traffic violator who the officer claimed appeared to be reaching for a gun. No gun was found. The Police Chief of Granville fired the officer the very next day and there were violent protests outside of the Police Department and the Courthouse. The officer was indicted for Murder by a Grand Jury and the case went to trial. A jury found the officer Not Guilty of all charges and the officer appealed his firing.

The second case was from Louisville, Kentucky. Two detectives entered an apartment to serve a warrant and one officer shot and killed one of the people in the apartment, who turned out to be unarmed. The Commonwealth Attorney, bowing to pressure from

Civil Rights leaders indicted the officer for Murder, but he too was found Not Guilty by a Jefferson County, Kentucky jury.

The third and fourth cases in the study were both from Cincinnati. In the first, a man who was wanted for assaulting a police officer ran when an officer, who recognized him, ordered him to stop. There was a foot pursuit and the suspect was tackled in a grassy area off the street. Officers claimed that the suspect violently resisted and the suspect was "hogtied" to secure him. The suspect was placed in the back of a police vehicle and stopped breathing. Attempts to re-start his breathing were unsuccessful and the suspect expired. The chasing officer was indicted on a Manslaughter charge. He too, was found Not Guilty. The next case resulted in the 2001 riots in Cincinnati. An officer, working off duty, saw a male wanted for outstanding traffic warrants and a foot chase ensued. The off duty officer ended his participation when an on duty officer started chasing the suspect. The chase went into a darkened alley and the officer fired a single shot killing the suspect, who he claimed was making a "furtive movement" as if reaching for a gun. The officer was charged with Negligent Homicide, a misdemeanor in Ohio, and the case was tried before a Judge at the request of the defendant. The Judge found the officer Not Guilty based upon the Graham standard.

The last case originated in Oakland, California where a Bay Area Regional Transit cop thought that he was reaching for his Taser to subdue a suspect, but instead pulled his 40 caliber handgun shooting the suspect once and killing him. The prosecutor in that case charged the officer with Voluntary Manslaughter and was able to get a conviction even though the requisite level of intent was clearly not there. The officer was clearly guilty of negligence, even though B.A.R.T. required him to carry his Taser directly behind his firearm.

The conclusion of the case study was that Prosecutors across the country consider the political correctness of charging when the case involves a law enforcement officer.

CHAPTER TWENTY-NINE

Dawn's parents wanted their daughter to have the perfect wedding and were sparing no expense for that to happen. St. Peter and Chains Catholic Church, the same church where funerals for cops have been held, and the reception would be in the ballroom of The Cincinnatian Hotel, where a wedding suite would be reserved for the new bride and groom.

As the date grew closer, Dawn appeared to be more and more antsy. She told Matt that she was not having second thoughts about marrying him, but that she wanted the day to be absolutely perfect. Matt was told to invite whoever he chose, but he had really not made a lot of friends since moving to Cincinnati. He invited a couple of cops that he had worked with and his mother and her male companion.

When they arrived at the church in a limo rented by Dawn's parents, Matt was shocked to see two lines of uniformed Cincinnati cops on the steps of the church. Matt almost broke down as the wedding couple walked up the steps to the salutes of the uniformed cops. As they passed by each pair of cops, the two cops fell in behind them and they developed a procession into the vestibule of the church. Matt was really uncomfortable being the center of attention, but the smile on his soon-to-be wife's face made it all worthwhile. He would later describe that smile to people as "the face on the kool aid pitcher." The ceremony went off without a hitch and the Priest stood behind Matt and Dawn and introduced them to the attendees as "Mr. and Mrs. Matthew Miles." They walked out of the church to two lines of cops facing each other with PR-24 nightsticks crossed in an arch. Matt was shocked to see that the last uniformed officer was Captain Newhall, who smacked Dawn's ass as she passed in the military tradition. The newlyweds were then taken in the limo to the hotel where they were met in the ballroom by a throng of well-wishers. They sat at the head table for a delicious dinner and then went back to their room to rest up for the reception. When they returned, the ballroom was rocking with the retired Lieutenant from the oldies station cranking out the hits. Matt got to dance with his mother and Dawn danced with her dad, then they had a dance to the song "Precious and Few" with each other. They cut the wedding cake, but had decided against slamming it into each other's face. Instead, they wrapped arms and fed the cake to each other. They decided to leave the party to the revelers and call it a night. They went up to their room and Dawn took a shower, returning in s silk teddy that she had bought just for this occasion. The two lovebirds rolled around on the king size bet, laughing and giggling like a couple of children, made love and then fell asleep in each other's arms.

***

When they awoke the following morning, they walked back to the apartment to begin their honeymoon. They had decided on a cruise to the southern tip of Mexico, but would make a circuitous drive to Miami to board the cruise. They drove south on I-75 to Knoxville, Tennessee, then east on I-40 to their first stopping point which was Ashville, North Carolina. They stayed overnight and then drove south on I-95 to Savannah, Georgia for another night of sightseeing and fun. The third day they arrived in Miami and boarded the cruise ship for a five day cruise.

***

The cruise ship was the length of four football fields and had four restaurants, three pools and a twenty-four hour casino operation. There was entertainment to be found on each of the seven levels of the ship, and a large elegant dining room for the passengers to eat.

On the first day out of port, Matt and Dawn marveled at the expanse of the Atlantic Ocean. Neither had ever been where there is no land to be seen in any direction for as far as the eye can see. The ship flowed along until the ship Captain announced that they had entered the Gulf of Mexico. The itinerary said that they would make five port stops, the first being late in the second day. Matt and Dawn went to the dining hall, which seated fifteen hundred people, for their dinner meal. The cruise had two seatings for the dinner meal to accommodate all of the passengers that it carried. They were taken to their table and marveled at all of the staff in their white jackets scurrying to meet the needs of the guests. As they awaited their first course, Matt saw four men in ski masks crash through the entry door into the dining area. All four held rifles and watched as the dining cheered for the show. There were several loud bangs and an announcement that the diners were being taken hostage. The guests in the room laughed and applauded the show, but Matt looked into the false ceiling and saw holes which told him they were firing live ammunition. Matt grabbed Dawn and pulled her under the table for protection. He reached into her purse and grabbed her .380 semi-automatic handgun as he whispered to her that this attack was REAL! Matt could see the right leg of one of the pirates from his position under the table, and remembered something that he learned in the Police Academy called the "bouncing bullet." A bullet fired at a hard surface will raise one to eight inches above that surface. Grabbing a seat cushion to muffle the sound of the gun firing, Matt fired one shot which struck the pirate in the ankle, causing him to scream out loudly. The other three men had no idea why their compatriot had dropped like a sack of potatoes or why he was grabbing his ankle, which was gushing blood.

***

Matt crawled to the nearest door and opened it only enough to slide out into the hallway. He moved slowly toward the main entrance when he heard footsteps running toward him. When the pirates turned the corner into his hallway, Matt fired two shots into the first and two more into the second, dropping them both to the floor dead. The fourth gunman ran, leaving his buddy bleeding and screaming on the floor of the dining room. Dawn jumped up and ran to the doorway, grabbing the pirate's AK-47 assault rifle and announcing to the diners in the hall that she is an American Police Officer. Matt and Dawn covered the two entrances to protect the diners and wait for help to arrive. After a little more than an hour, they saw four men in tactical attire with an American flag on the shoulder enter the area and yell, "United States Navy, we are here to protect you!" From her position off to the side of the entry way, Dawn also yelled, "Cincinnati, Ohio Police Officer, my husband is on your left!" She held her badge high in the air so the SEALS would see it. Matt came out of his hidden area and laid down Dawn's .380, which now only had three bullets left in the magazine. He told the SEALS that there were two men down in the hallway and that both were dead. Two of the SEALS peeled off to verify the information while one of the SEALS tended to the wounds of the last pirate. None of the diners had moved an inch as they watched the movements of the two cops and military personnel.

The SEALS told Matt and Dawn that a US warship had received a distress call from the Captain saying that Somali pirates had boarded the ship and were attempting to get control. The SEALS repelled down from a helicopter after the chopper fired on the pirates boat and they had surrendered. They said they captured one pirate running back toward his boat, and that they now understood why he was running.

The Captain of the ship arrived in the dining area and walked up onto the stage to tell the passengers that they were safe. He was still unaware of the heroics of Matt and Dawn until one of the people in the front row yelled that they had been saved by two American police officers. The Captain summoned Matt and Dawn onto the stage where they received a standing ovation from the 1,500 passengers in the room.

Matt and Dawn sat at the Captain's table as his personal guest and the cruise line returned the price of the cruise.

CHAPTER THIRTY

When Matt and Dawn returned to Cincinnati they learned that Dawn's grievance had been upheld and that she was being transferred to District Two on the eight pm to six am power shift. That would work out well for both as she would be sleeping while he was in class and he would have evenings free to prepare for the moot court, graduation and the bar examination.

***

Matt was disappointed when he received his term paper back with a b minus grade. The professor wrote on the paper that Matt's conclusion was not supported by this cases he cited. Matt knew that the professor's liberal bias toward police would cause him consternation, but was still hurt because his cases clearly established and justified his conclusions. He remembered that, as someone had said, "Never let facts get in the way of ideology."

***

Matt directed all of his efforts into preparing for the moot court. He had chosen a twenty-six year old female third year student who impressed him because she was willing to go the mat with professors with whom she disagreed. She appeared to be extremely well versed in Civil Rules of Procedure as well and that would be important at trial. The other student he chose was an articulate twenty-five year old male who showed an extreme interest in researching case law and wowing the professors. The case they were handed was representing Proctor & Gamble, who were the Defendants in a product liability case involving their over one hundred year old soap. The Plaintiff in the case claimed that the soap damaged her skin to the point of requiring plastic surgery and argued that the case should be given class action status so other plaintiffs could jump on board. The case had been won in the trial court and was now on appeal.

The team would have fifteen minutes to argue their case. Because they would now have the burden of proof that the decision of the trial court was wrong, they would get the first and last word. Their opponents from the University of Cincinnati would get their fifteen minutes in the middle and have the opportunity to challenge whatever Matt chose to present in his first segment.

The three met nightly for two hours strategizing their presentation. They decided to challenge the granting of the status of class action in the first portion, causing the UC student lawyers to address that issue with their time, and then go after the facts of the one plaintiff's case when they could not be challenged.

Each student was assigned a task. Matt would present the final argument on the facts, the female would present the first portion and the third member was tasked with finding case law from other courts to support their position and writing the brief that the Judges would read prior to oral arguments.

Their plan worked with precision as the decision of the three Appellate Court Justices was unanimous in reversing the lower court decision, meaning Xavier won the contest.

The Dean of Xavier Law acknowledged the great work of all three of his students and took them to dinner at a swank restaurant downtown. The Dean pulled Matt off to the side and told him that one of the Judges had made an offer to let Matt work as a law clerk for him if he was interested.

CHAPTER THIRTY-ONE

Matt saw his graduation from Law School as a blessing because the course work had taken its toll on his sanity. Although he had hoped to be the Class Valedictorian, someone else was given that honor. Matt sat at the graduation ceremony listening to this man who clearly had a strong belief that all cops were just plain bad. It was actually ironic that a white male would be railing on the ills of black males and the police. His references to Ferguson, Missouri; Cleveland, Ohio; and Staten Island, New York were so far left that Matt just blocked it out and waited for the ceremony to end. He went so far as to mention the Trayvon Martin case in his diatribe, which was intriguing since the shooter, George Zimmerman, was neither white nor a cop.

The next step was to prepare for the bar examination, which has a first time pass rate of approximately thirty percent. The test is only given in Columbus, Ohio, so Matt arrived two days early and secluded himself in his hotel room without television and strict orders of no telephone calls. The test to become an attorney is broken into three parts: tax law, civil law and criminal law. Each requires a minimum seventy percent score to pass. If any phase is failed, the person only need re-take that portion at a later date. Once all three sections are passed, the person is sworn in by the Ohio Supreme Court and is authorized to practice law in Ohio. If the attorney wishes to practice in other states as well, he or she must take and pass their examinations individually. Matt arrived home to find Dawn sitting at the dining room table sipping on a cup of tea. She looked at him and didn't even ask how he fared on the test. Instead, she showed a very forlorn look on her face as she announced, "the rabbit DIED!" She gleefully told him that he was going to be a daddy.

CHAPTER THIRTY-TWO

Dawn's pregnancy was in the late stages and Matt suggested she put in for light duty. Dawn declined saying she would continue to pull her weight and then take maternity leave when she felt that she was unable to physically perform her duties. Matt kissed her goodbye as she left for her shift, told her he loved her and told her to be safe.

***

Matt was sleeping soundly when the entry buzzer began sounding wildly. Thinking that Dawn had forgotten her door key again, Matt tried to sound like a ghoul into the speaker when he said, "Can I help you?" A male voice came through the speaker saying, "This is Coronel Paul Henries, would you let me in please?"

***

Panic set in immediately as Matt hit the release to open the outer door. An Assistant Police Chief would not be at his door if Dawn had been hurt, they would have sent a beat cop. Matt was waiting at his door as the Assistant Chief and another uniformed cop got off the elevator. Matt let the two cops into the apartment and slumped down on the couch. Henries sat down in a chair while the other officer stood silently near the door. The Assistant Chief told Matt that Dawn and her partner answered a domestic call at Bramble and Whetzel Avenue at approximately two-ten am. When they got to the intersection with two other marked units, the three cars were ambushed by automatic rifle fire. Dawn was killed instantly from a shot to the head, her partner, Officer Dave Eisley suffered a gunshot that entered between his bulletproof vest collapsing his right lung and the two other police cars were shot up and their drivers were wounded. There were a total of twenty-seven shots that hit Dawn's police vehicle and it was clearly a planned ambush. The Chief went on to say that emergency room doctors authorized the paramedics to remove the baby from Dawn's stomach in order to try to try to save it, but their heroic efforts were unsuccessful and the baby was declared dead at the hospital. The look of disbelief on Matt's face told the whole story. The Chief went on to say that the suspects had escaped and that a countywide manhunt was underway to capture them. The evidence at the scene showed a minimum of two shooters and likely three. After a short period of eerie silence, Matt asked where Dawn's body had been taken. The Chief replied simply, "The County Morgue. We will take you there if that is what you want." Matt nodded and got up from the couch to get dressed.

***

Dawn's body was on a slab at the County Morgue when Matt and his escorts arrived. The attendant only pulled the sheet covering her down to the next because her stomach had been cut open to remove the fetus. Matt stared at his wife blankly and bent down to kiss her forehead before turning and walking out of the room. The Chief told Matt softly, "Your police family will be with you every step of the way. Officer Seemoan is on her way here and will remain with you to offer and help she can. I know that she was your FTO and that you trust her."

***

Liza arrived about twenty minutes later in her personal car and told Matt she was taking him home. When they arrived at Matt and Dawn's apartment, she removed and overnight bag from the trunk of her car and told Matt she would be sleeping on his couch. She tried to console Matt as best she could because he was sobbing uncontrollably. They went into the apartment and she made them coffee because it would clearly be a long day. Matt and Liza sat and talked about their early days together and the little she knew about Dawn's career with the Police Department. A little after seven am, the door buzzer sounded and it was one of the Police Department chaplain's, a Catholic Priest whose radio call number was 6God10. The Priest told Matt that he would assist with the arrangements for Dawn's funeral. Matt told the chaplain that he and Dawn had not considered burial plots and did not have a clue what to do. The Priest called The Archdiocese of Cincinnati office and set up for three side-by-side plots at a Catholic cemetery in St. Bernard, a city in the middle of Cincinnati. The Priest then made arrangements with a funeral home to pick up the bodies of Dawn and the unborn daughter, who still had not been given a name and set up for St. Peter in Chains to conduct the funeral mass for them. He talked with Matt about a name for the baby and Matt decided on Kelly, Dawn's mother's name. He said Dawn would approve of that name. The

Police Department delivered a full dress uniform to the funeral home that Dawn would be buried in. She would be wearing her badge and that number would be forever retired. There was little sleep for Matt and Liza, who never left his side. Matt was having a difficult time keeping his composure, but Liza was always there to comfort him. Matt's mother and her companion were at the apartment on a regular basis, as were Dawn's mom and dad. The layout would be on Tuesday from four until nine pm with a private viewing for family only after. The funeral would be at ten am on Wednesday. Liza drove Matt to the funeral home at three pm on Tuesday afternoon. When they arrived there were literally hundreds of cops in uniform milling around for their chance to pay their respects to a fallen hero. There was a reception area set up and a uniformed police officer at each end of casket standing as an honor guard. The parents flanked Matt and Liza stood directly behind Matt in case he became overwhelmed.

***

The line outside continued to grow and now was around one thousand. They would enter single file and stop at the open casket to pay final respects and then pass the family. The first group to enter were from Concerns of Police Survivors (COPS), a group made up of spouses and loved ones of police officers who died in the line of duty. That included the wives of Cincinnati officers who died up to thirty years earlier. Matt was shocked when a British bobby wearing the traditional large hat stopped and gave his condolences. A police officer from Ontario Provincial Police in Canada and an Assistant Police Chief from the New South Wales, Australia Police passed by as well. Law enforcement agencies from every corner of the continental United States had sent at least one representative to show their solidarity with a fallen comrade. Nine o'clock came and went with a line of officers still waiting their chance to pass by Dawn's casket. It was almost eleven when the doors finally closed and Matt was given private time with his wife and child. It had been decided that the child should be buried with his mother rather than in a separate coffin. She would forever be holding the child on her left shoulder and they would travel to Heaven together. After a few minutes of being alone with her, the rest of the family got to say their last goodbyes to Dawn and the child.

***

The morning brought rain and a chill in the air as the procession to the church was led for four police motorcycles. Two were Cincinnati, one was the University of Cincinnati, and the last was the Hamilton County Sheriff. When the procession arrived at the front entrance of the church, there were literally thousands of cops lining the street and Matt cringed when he saw a new police academy class in two lines up the steps to the entrance, just as his class had been when he and Dawn were in the academy together. The recruits jumped to attention and saluted as the casket was carried up the steps by the pall bearers. Matt took a moment to look at the sea of uniformed cops, all standing at attention and saluting to honor his wife's service. Matt was asked if he wanted to say anything to the throngs of people about his wife. When he said that he did, he was told that he would speak after the Mayor of Cincinnati and the Chief of Police. When it was his turn to speak, Matt walked slowly to the microphone and spoke without a prepared text. He told the packed church, "All of the people who knew Dawn knew that she was an extraordinary woman. In the end, she did nothing more than every officer attending this service would do. She gave her life to make the lives of others safe. The outpouring of love and support from civilians who did not know either of us cannot be expressed in words. I thank you for your service as much as you are here to thank my wife for hers. I know that the gates of heaven opened wide when she arrived, as they have for the heroic police officers who arrived there before her. May you all travel with God's speed."

***

The casket was carried from the church to the yell of ATTENTION by a Cincinnati Assistant Police Chief, and as he had done before, the recruits dropped their salute in perfect harmony as the casket passed each pair. The procession went thru downtown Cincinnati and headed north on Vine with uniformed cops and just plain people saluting and waving American flags as the hearse passed. No one seemed to care that the streets were closed during lunch hour on a business day. This inconvenience was worth it! As they proceeded up Vine Street Hill en route to the cemetery, Matt took a moment to turn around and look out the back window of the limo. As far as he could see back down the hill were two lines of police cars with their red and blue lights flashing silently. In fact, the last car in the procession had not left the church as the motorcycles were entering the cemetery, a distance of just over four miles. As the procession entered the cemetery there were two fire trucks draped with an American flag attached to their ladders crossed for the procession to pass under. Roger Bacon High School, a Catholic school directly across the street from the cemetery, had their entire student body standing in silent awe of the event they were witnessing. The Hamilton County Sheriff's Bagpipe Corps led the flag draped casket to its final resting place. There was a significant delay in the service because the procession was continuing to arrive. The Priest, who had been at Matt's home, blessed Dawn's final resting place. There was a final call from Police Communications to Dawn. The countywide tones dropped and police officers from Ohio, Kentucky and Indiana heard the following: "Attention all cars all departments, an all-county broadcast. Cincinnati communications to Car 2411. Cincinnati communications to Car 2411. Cincinnati communications to Officer Dawn Taylor-Miles. Officer Dawn Taylor Miles is 27 forever, may she rest in Peace." That was immediately followed by the playing of Taps and a twenty-one gun salute. The flag was then carefully removed from the casket, folded and then handed to the Police Chief, who carefully handed it to Matt. The service had ended.

CHAPTER THIRTY-THREE

It was a little after two am when Matt got up off the couch and walked to the dining room table. He sat down and scribbled a note on a sheet of paper, folding the paper and placing it in his shirt pocket. He put on his coat, placing something in the right pocket, grabbed his car keys and walked out the door. Matt drove back to Mount Echo Park and sat on the same bench overlooking the Ohio River as he had when he resigned from the Police Department. He pulled Dawn's .380 from his jacket and fired one round into his right temple killing him instantly. He lay slumped in the bench for almost two hours until a sixteen year old boy noticed him while riding his bike in the park. The boy picked up the .380 and rode away. It was daylight when two joggers came upon the body and called the police. Detective Weeman found the note in Matt's shirt pocket. It said simply, "I lost everything with the death of my wife and child. I have nothing left to live for."

EPILOGUE

The character in this book is obviously fictional, but many of the situations involving law enforcement were based on actual events. A young police officer, on his first day of patrolling alone, actually responded to an apartment building to find a beheaded 23 year old female, as described in the book and a police officer did actually die when he fell from a vehicle, which dragged him several blocks. Law enforcement sees both the best and worst of people on a daily basis. The final chapter was the most difficult to write because it embodies the sense of loss suffered by law enforcement all over the United States for a brother or sister that they have never met. The true loss of a police officer in the line of duty is a loss to the society as a whole. This book pays homage to the brave men and women who are willing to risk their very existence to assure that others have a safe environment to live, work and play.